The Complete Guide for
THE
ANXIOUS
GROOM

*How to Avoid Everything That Could
Go Wrong on Her Big Day*

Steven Lewis

New Page Books
A division of Career Press, Inc.
Franklin Lakes, NJ

Copyright © 2004 by Steven Lewis

All rights reserved under the Pan-American and International Copyright Conventions. This book may not be reproduced, in whole or in part, in any form or by any means electronic or mechanical, including photocopying, recording, or by any information storage and retrieval system now known or hereafter invented, without written permission from the publisher, The Career Press.

>THE COMPLETE GUIDE FOR THE ANXIOUS GROOM
EDITED BY AND TYPESET BY KATE HENCHES
Cover design by Cheryl Cohan Finbow
Cover Photograph by Gary Jung
Formal wear for cover courtesy of Varsity Formal Wear
807 Franklin Ave., Franklin Lakes, NJ 07417, *varsitytuxedos.com*
Printed in the U.S.A. by Book-mart Press

To order this title, please call toll-free 1-800-CAREER-1 (NJ and Canada: 201-848-0310) to order using VISA or MasterCard, or for further information on books from Career Press.

CAREER PRESS

New Page BOOKS

The Career Press, Inc., 3 Tice Road, PO Box 687,
Franklin Lakes, NJ 07417
www.careerpress.com
www.newpagebooks.com

Library of Congress Cataloging-in-Publication Data

Lewis, Steven M.
   The complete guide for the anxious groom : how to avoid everything that could go
  wrong on her big day / by Steven Lewis.
     p. cm.
  Includes index.
  ISBN 1-56414-747-9 (pbk.)
    1. Bridegrooms. 2. Weddings—Planning. 3. Wedding etiquette. 4. Betrothal.
I. Title.

HQ745.L49 2004
395.2'2--dc22

2004040877

Dedication

To my wife, Patricia, of course.
She's still the one.

For Danny and Bay.

And decades down the road,
for Clay, Devin, Connor, Rory,
and whatever other boys brighten our lives.

Acknowledgments

I would like to thank Arlene Dubin, Betty and George Gaynor, my old pal Richard Gaynor, Mike Halminski, Ruth Hayden, Julie Isaacson, Andrew Kossover, Dr. Cynthia Pizzulli, Stacey Sheeley, Dr. Marj Steinfeld, Tricia Townsend, the fine people at prenupKit.com, the California Society of CPAs, and all the really good-spirited contributors to this project.

Special thanks to Ed Knappman at New England Publishing Associates.

Contents

Introduction   9

Part I: Warm-Ups

Chapter 1: Lacing Up Your Sneakers   15
Checking in with your future father-in-law and asking his blessing—not his okay.

Chapter 2: Grabbing the Championship Ring   25
Some good, solid, unambiguous, man-to-man advice about choosing the ring of your girlfriend's dreams

Chapter 3: The Playbook   37
Eight Fill-in-the Blank Proposal Scripts

Chapter 4: The Real World of Engagement Stories   51
Real people tell real engagement stories.

Part II: The Long Season: The Engagement Year(s)

Chapter 5: The Give and Go   69
Some reflections on maleness, duty, work, partnership, political correctness, and above all, love.

Chapter 6: The Game Plan   77
Step-by-step preparations for any wedding of any size or style.

Chapter 7: Contract Time   93
What the whole deal costs in real dollars and pounds of flesh.

Chapter 8: The Xs and Os   107
Your financial and legal rights and responsibilities.

Chapter 9: 10 Taboos for the Bachelor Party   **123**
The 10 big don'ts.

Chapter 10: Shooting For the (Honey)Moon   **131**

Part III: June Madness

Chapter 11: A Gentle Reminder: **149**
Some reflections on the ineffable magic of love and marriage.

Chapter 12: Weddiquette   **157**
Includes the 11 reasons why it's definitely not cool to push wedding cake in your bride's face.

Chapter 13: Sex and the Not-So-Single Single Guy   **165**
How to turn the pressure of the wedding night into the pleasure of each other's company.

Chapter 14: Going to the Line   **175**
Testimonials From men and women who have been there.

Part IV: Post-Game Wrap-Up

Chapter 15: The First Day of the Rest of Your Married Life   **189**
Talking the talk; walking the walk;
and laughing all the way home.

Chapter 16: What Makes a Perfect Husband   **201**
Married and divorced women tell you what it takes.

Afterword   **211**

Appendix: Crunching the Numbers   **213**
Price charts for diamonds.

Index   **217**

About the Author   **223**

Introduction

It's been more than 35 years since I slipped on the existential banana peel and breathlessly hitched my lucky star to the smart and sexy Patti Henderson of New Orleans, Louisiana. Frankly, I still don't know how it happened. But here's the rough-cut chronology:

1. April Something, 1968: I am an unfocused, unkempt, underachieving three-time dropout from the University of Wisconsin. I am also desperately in love with a girl from the Deep South whom I had first kissed just a few wintry months before. With absolutely nothing to offer my new love except the promise of a most unpromising future with a poet, I ask her (or maybe it was beg her) to suspend her better judgment and spend the rest of her days with me, a 21-year-old New York Jew with no degree, no career to speak of, and no foreseeable prospects. Lord knows why, but she says yes.

2. A 60-second kiss later, panicked that she will change her mind in another 60 seconds, I lead her by the hand around the narrow cobbled streets of Cambridge, Massachusetts, and into a secondhand shop where I pull every cent I own from the lint in my frayed jeans pocket and buy an antique opal ring. We are thus unofficially, officially engaged.

3. August 25, 1968: Patti and I follow her mother's detailed instructions and take the ferry from New Orleans across the Mississippi River to Algiers to get a blood test, for what

I honestly do not know. (Back then states required all newlyweds to get tested for syphilis and gonnorhea.)

4. August 28, 1968: Although the previous 48 hours are pretty much a complete haze from the intense Delta humidity and all the Jim Beam I consumed down in the Quarter, I know from the photographs that at some point I must have submitted to a homemade haircut and later managed to slip into a white linen suit (purchased by my father-in-law). I also apparently stepped into my best hipster brown boots and had my troth plighted in front of assembled friends and family in the Henderson's living room, Dr. James DeLando, officiating. That's about it.

To merely state that I was an ignorant participant in what has turned out to be the most important day in my life would be to grossly underestimate how fortunate I am that Patti Henderson is still my wife. And frankly, so it was with all of my friends from back then…most of whom, I should tell you, are long divorced.

So much has changed in this country during the three decades since Patti and I were mispronounced "man and wife." Our seven children have grown up in a country that has almost driven the length of the court in terms of changing attitudes about gender equality. Without underestimating the great accomplishments in areas such as medicine and space travel (and let's not forget Viagra), I don't think there has been anything as important as the way we have come to view the relationship between men and women.

However, judging by the utter bewilderment my oldest son Cael brought to his own engagement and wedding—and, more recently, my sons-in-law Michael, Jon, and Jeffrey—it's also become quite clear that despite all the raising of consciousness of the past three decades, all the heightened awareness apparently did a flying leap over the marriage altar.

From those anxious moments before the male knee hits the floor and the stuttering question has been popped (or the mutually agreed upon terms of the union have been settled over glasses of merlot), the control and disposition of the marital season has been wired into the tenacious bi-generational grasp of the bride and her mother—or the sometimes indecipherable manifestations of a wedding coordinator named Franz.

More often than not, the future groom is as clueless as his father once was about the duties and responsibilities of the male partner in the wedding. And after all is said and done (without him ever having said or done much of anything), he is the one standing to the side of the wedding aisle smiling thinly and waiting impatiently for his bride to show up so he can finally say what he's been told to say in his own words.

That scenario might have worked well enough for his dad, but as we've come to learn in the two-career, shared-annuity real world of 2004, it is only common sense to take an active and thoughtful role in perhaps the most meaningful event in anyone's life. It's not wise—or satisfying—to be a silent partner in any merger that is supposed to last "all the days of your life."

In retrospect, the engagement season of my oldest son Cael is wonderful example: Before he asked sweet Melissa to share the rest of his life, had he considered such important issues as prenups, life and health insurance, eternal cohabitation (including sharing a bathroom with a female), children, checkbooks, in-laws, and the countless other concerns with which unmarried men are wise to concern themselves before getting hitched? I don't think so. In his mind, he was just getting married—and then going on a pleasure-filled cruise in the Caribbean.

As his father, I take substantial blame for this example of late 20th century mindlessness. A dad has certain well-defined responsibilities to groom his sons for manhood and, I might add, groomhood. At the risk of sounding a little smug, I think I did fairly well with most of those thorny manhood issues. However, in this one, somewhat narrow, groom area (with some rather non-narrow implications), I was completely worthless, essentially as unprepared for my son's wedding as I was for my own.

And thus this attempt at redemption.

Rene Zellwegger says of Tom Cruise in *Jerry Maguire*, "I love him for the man that he wants to be, and I love him for the man that he almost is." *The Complete Guide for the Anxious Groom* will take a load of myth and misinformation off your shoulders and will allow you to be the groom you want to be—and the husband you almost are.

P.S. If you've already taken care of all the pre-season stuff—the dad, the ring, and the knee—just skip ahead to Chapter 4. As the great British basketball player John Locke once wrote, "No man's knowledge here can go beyond his experience."

Part I
Warm-Ups

Chapter 1

Lacing Up Your Sneakers

Pre-season rule: Ask for her father's blessing, not his approval. It doesn't matter that "it really doesn't matter." It matters. Ask him and then get out of the way. It's a kind of a give and go.

The history of suitors asking the intended bride's father for his blessing goes all the way back to ancient (and less ancient) times when women were considered chattel. Clearly—and thankfully—in our development as a civilized people we have moved well beyond such perverse and demeaning transactions. Nevertheless, there remains in our cultural consciousness an unwavering emotional belief that a father's role in life is very much tied to protecting his children—especially his female children. Agree with it or not, that belief remains a real force to be reckoned with into the present age and beyond. I not only believe you can reckon with it forcefully and effectively (and not lose any pride in the transaction), but that it will work in your best interest in the long run.

Anyone who is considering dropping this formality as an outmoded ritual should try to remember the scowl behind the smile on all the faces of all the fathers of all the daughters he has dated. He might also read Shakespeare's "Othello" for some insight into the ways in which fathers think men steal their little girls—or Arthur Miller's *View From the Bridge* to see a dramatic representation of how murderous the process can get.

When Do You Pop the Pop Question?

Should you speak to her old man *before* you get down on your knee and ask his daughter to share your bed for the rest of her life or *after*? Tough one. Fake left and go left...or fake left and go right? Some people will advise talking to the dad before you actually go out and purchase the ring and pop the question. They say it's the only way a skeptical father will feel that you are truly asking for his blessing and will seriously consider his wishes.

Others say that asking the dad for his blessing is a mere formality, one that shows respect for her father's position and his feelings, but carries no promise or intention to heed his wishes. They say that asking him before asking her could be construed as rather disrespectful to the intended partner.

Frankly, I don't think it matters. In truth, either is fine and both are acceptable.

Whatever you decide, though, I think the important things for you to do are:

1. Let him know that you are man enough to be a good husband to his daughter—you don't want to give her father (or anyone) the power over your marriage. Doing so puts you in a decidedly weak and dependent position— one that he might initially like, but will eventually leave him disdainful of you.
2. Make it clear that you are not asking his permission, but rather you are asking for his blessing on your intention of stealing the poor man's daughter right out from under his wing.

If he says yes, then go speak with her. And if he says no, then go speak with her. You've done your duty.

What Do You Say?

No big stories, no long prefaces. Most men don't want to get all touchy-feely when they're being asked to give up the only people in the world who think they can do no wrong—their little girls. Your future father-in-law's wife knows exactly what kind of man he is—and loves him anyway. His sons, in becoming men themselves, have also taken a measure of the man and love him for how he tried to raise them into men. But his daughter loves him for the man whose feet she danced on, whose arms carried her to bed when she fell asleep on the couch, who would make an absolute ass out of himself if he even thought she was in some danger.

So, take a deep breath and let him know the only three things that he truly wants to hear:

1. You love his daughter with all your heart.
2. You will do everything in your power to make her happy.
3. You will never do anything to hurt her.

After that, if he doesn't kill you, you're in like Flynn (whatever the hell that means).

Grand Theft Auto

If Michael had just given me some kind of warning, some of that unspoken communication between men that we're so good at, I know I would have made it easy for him. Or at least easier. I would have put an arm around his much-bigger-than-my-own shoulders and made some sort of joke. I would have greased the aisle, so to speak. I like him. Always have (especially after he passed with flying colors my rigorous 60 day test in 1991 about the underlying intentions of boyfriends—see *Zen and the Art of Fatherhood* [Dutton, 1997]). But, frankly, I was as lost as he was, belted into the passenger seat of a no-year VW Rabbit (with a Budweiser logo on the hood) as Nancy's boyfriend, Michael Domitrovits, transported me to the Raleigh-Durham airport.

Although I had known Michael since he was in peewee league soccer in our upstate New York town—and he had been "officially" dating Nancy since they were seniors at New Paltz Central High School—I naturally assumed that he did not relish the idea of being trapped in a speeding steel cage with his girlfriend's father for 30 long, and silently sweaty, minutes. No man, young or old, is ever comfortable with the eternally scowling father of his present squeeze, regardless of whether the father is scowling. (Fathers of daughters are *always* scowling behind those smiles.) And although I had told him on several occasions since 1991 that it was all right to call me Steve, he still could do no better than "Ahem" in 1997.

So, I thought I'd make the half-hour drive easy for the poor guy. This meant that I started yammering the moment I dropped my fatherly bulk into the hard, springy seat and shut the padless door. I talked sports cars. I talked Clemson football (he had recently graduated from the school). I talked Black Crowes. I talked Dell Computers. I talked ACC basketball. I talked Bill Clinton, Homer Simpson, Jack Nicholson, Shaquille O'Neal...I talked so much man-talk that the kid didn't have to say one word from 15–501 to the first Research Triangle exits off I-40 (about 10 miles), his head bobbing up and down like one of those Packer dummies in the back of cars all over Wisconsin, his tongue licking his lips. And I still had a thin but useful mental portfolio of subjects that I could carry over to the next time we drove somewhere together.

At one point, just before we reached the airport exit, my mouth had gotten so dry from the non-stop palaver I had to stop talking momentarily and find some saliva so that I could start up all the yammering again. At that point I figured I was one subject shy of rolling right up to the Midway entrance at the terminal. It was the only time I stopped talking, though.

Trapped Inside
of Mobile With Those Memphis Blues Again

And that was when Michael finally stopped nodding his head and uttered a sound—kind of a low moan—like a cow that had eaten too much sweet spring grass.

"Ya know...," he lowed, a breathy pause for the name he still couldn't speak, "I've been meaning to ask you, ya know, a question, ya know, for some time now...."

Yeah, like 30 minutes of listening to your girlfriend's father prattle on and on.

"Shoot," I smiled, pleased that I might not have to use all my conversation ammo in one blast. I was ready for practically anything: sports, cars, medical, finances, whatever. Anything but what kind of condom I use.

"Well, um, I was thinking, um, that I want to ask Nancy to marry me and..."

(To this day I'm not sure if the gasp that followed was silent, but the busted muffler on the Rabbit was probably loud enough to drown out my desperate coughing for oxygen.)

"...and I was hoping you'd give me your blessing...."

Michael cranked his head around as if he was in mid-exorcism. His green complexion making it look as though he had stopped breathing on the spot in anticipation of the archetypal paternal explosion that includes sampling of any of the following metal shards: *What the hell do you have to offer her? How much do you make? Have you read Shakespeare? Do you know Sharon Olds' poetry? Do you know what an annuity is? Do you have insurance? You probably think you're better than me! I mean, just who the hell do you think you are? And just what the f*** are your intentions?*

Of course I didn't say any of that. Or I hope I didn't. But as the man who just a moment before had more words to spew than time to spew them, I was suddenly rendered incapable of uttering a syllable. Or a squeak. In a span that probably lasted all of three seconds but felt like three fully catatonic hours, all I could think was, *We are both going to die in a firey crash if I don't figure out how to get that boy breathing again.*

I smiled again, but in retrospect I suspect it was the g-forces of the Rabbit going 140 mph around the cloverleaf exit, pulling my fluttering cheeks back against my bony face. "Michael... you don't need my blessing," I finally coughed out, lifting my arm in slow-mo and laying my hand on his shoulder like a defrocked priest.

I watched as his rigid face turned from green to white, his hands knuckled and shaking on the steering wheel, "But you certainly have it...."

This was when he lifted his lead foot from the accelerator, his face instantly began to pink up and he finally started to brake. *Thank God.*

That's the last thing I remember that day. I suppose that I actually got on the airplane without incident because I did eventually arrive in Newburgh and drove home to our house in the woods without a police escort.

That's it. But it's not all.

It's important that I tell you here how appreciative I've come to be for the simple act of Michael asking for my blessing. Not my approval; he didn't need that. And not my permission; he's not my child. In truth, it never actually occurred to me that any boy would ask for my blessing. I had always figured that was reserved for *The Godfather* movies. But in the moment that Michael popped the pre-popping question, his stock rose immeasurably in my eyes. In my cluelessness, I recognized it instantly as a gesture between men that goes back eons and pays a certain homage to the uniquely ambiguous relationship a father has with a daughter.

Although it is probably not acceptable to say this in certain circles today, the joy that a dad feels at seeing his daughter grow up and find true love is matched only by the utter shock that she would ever grow up at all and love anyone else but him. There's nothing to be done about it, of course, but it's true nevertheless. And so the not-so-simple act of asking for a father's "blessing" is no more—and no less—than a tacit acknowledgement by the asker that this is one mother of a transition for her father, and if the soon-to-be-groom wants the old man to get out of his way, he better do it well and do it respectfully. I respect that.

That said, Michael's Xs and Os could have been altered a bit to make the transition a little less anxious and far less life-threatening. Sitting shoulder to shoulder in a speeding Rabbit might have cut too close to the bone. Besides being dangerous, there's nowhere to go—other than over a cliff—if her dad sneers at you and growls, "Not over my dead body!"

The Ambush

In retrospect, the blessing Michael wished for certainly would have been accomplished with considerably less sweat and a whole lot more oxygen if he had just given me some kind of warning—maybe a vague invitation for a beer or a cup of coffee (the unspoken call for a *mano a mano*), or a message on the answering machine at work (made when he knew I wasn't there). He could have at least snuck up from behind rather than from the side.

From behind is the way Addie's boyfriend, Jon, ambushed me a few months after Michael nearly propelled me off that particular cliff.

It was during Christmas vacation. The house was full of kids and dogs and games and crumpled paper and people I didn't recognize, and while everyone else was in the living room watching the games, Jon remained suspiciously behind in the kitchen, just sittin' there on a stool at the counter while I was washing the dishes. We were jawing the way that men jaw aimlessly about things instantly forgettable when I heard what I thought was that same old painful mooing a few paces behind me.

Hot water scalding my hands, I held my breath and waited. And then, just as I could have lip-synched it, the lowing turned into a scratchy voice saying, "Ya know, I've been meaning to, ya know, ask you...a question...."

The primordial gurgle that escaped my lungs was nothing if not private, directed right at the frosty kitchen window and muffled by my shaking paws slurping around in the soapy water. And because my back was turned, I had ample time to clamp my eyes shut, check to see if I was having a nightmare, turn off the faucet and dry my hands on a towel before pivoting to face my fate. (And at the same time Jon could take three precautionary breaths and calm himself down before he started to throw up.)

So when I finally turned and looked indirectly into the eyes of my second future son-in-law (actually somewhere over his right shoulder) and said my lines, it didn't appear like I was homicidal—or suicidal. And Jon didn't have that remarkable green patina that I will forever associate with poor Michael's face. And, of course, we weren't going 140 mph around a cloverleaf.

I caught my breath, inhaled deeply through my nose to puff out my chest, and offered my blessings. A few seconds later he walked unsteadily around the kitchen island and we hugged like men, bumping chests and delivering the three requisite open-handed slaps on the back with the right hand.

The Three Card Monty

Then there was Jeffrey. Jeffrey Trapani had been Clover's squeeze on and off since 8th grade (when he wrote "Crimson and Clover, over and over," 1,800 times in his notebook). He tried a completely different but equally surprising tactic.

Jeffrey showed up alone and unannounced at the house one Saturday afternoon. Clover was in Boston and Jeffrey was in for a few days to see his family. I was just about to leave the house and go to the hardware store in town—and Patti was working in the garden. (I know, I know, it doesn't get any more mom-and-pop than that!)

Anyway, my first thought when I saw him pull up the long driveway through the woods was, *Poor Jeffrey thinks he has to make an obligatory visit just because he's in town for a few days!* Then I thought, *How nice that he feels comfortable enough to just stop by—even if it's totally out of obligation.* (I, for one, would never ever have stopped in on a girlfriend's parents for any reason, ever, if she wasn't right by my side.) Finally, I decided that he just wanted to revisit the living room couch upon which he spent so many happy high school hours back in the early 90s. That was all before my dogs barked and ran circles around his car and the cats raced to jump up on the hood.

You'd think that I would have had it figured out by then, but no...I offered him a beer, which he declined (which should have alerted me that something was up) and then we chatted law school over the same kitchen counter Jon lobbed his volleys at me. The Red Sox and Yankees, rents in Boston, crime in Jamaica Plains, his lunatic dog Bella Luna, local gossip, family gossip, Dick Cheney driving the country into hell in a handbasket...a thousand and one things were pitched, but nothing leading anywhere, and all the while wondering when the other shoe is going to drop.

In my confusion and mounting desperation to get to the hardware store, I was going to offer a beer again, but I checked my watch...4:30...suddenly realizing that I had to leave within five minutes to get to the hardware store before it closed.

My initial escape plan, because Jeffrey was clearly sticking around for the long haul (maybe he was hoping for some of Patti's red beans and rice?) was to lure him outside and then palm him off on my wife.

The luring was easy. The palming, not so easy. Patti was being no help, pretty much ignoring both of us as we stood staring at her on the other side of the fence. We stood uneasily in the thick grass outside the garden fence pushing the forced conversation along the way a man leans into a push power going up hill when I finally gave up and blurted out, "I gotta run or I'm gonna miss..." when Jeffrey's face turned bright red and he blurted out, "Before you go, I just have an important question I need to ask you...."

Suddenly the lightbulb went on—*aha!* But rather than act my age and lead the obviously nervous guy over to some lawn chairs, I laughed right out loud..."So that's what this whole thing has been all about!"

He nodded a little sheepishly.

And here again I missed my cue: Rather than letting him speak the speech he had rehearsed all the way from Boston, I said, "Of course you have my blessing..." and then laughed some more and then we did the traditional man hug.

Jeffrey looked relieved that it was over, but ultimately a little unsatisfied that he didn't get a chance to do what he thought was right and proper.

Some Man-to-Man Alternatives

An effective alternative to variations of the Grand Theft Auto, the Ambush, or the Three Card Monty, is to invite your future father-in-law out to lunch or just out for a beer. First, he's going to know it's a setup and as such will have time to prepare himself for whatever you're going to toss his way. And second, the invitation situation provides a wonderful opportunity for you to maintain some degree of autonomy and control (by picking up the check) while still showing a certain humility and respect for his age and position.

Two side-by-side stools in a tavern are perfect. They provide a good bit of room for both uncomfortable men to maneuver—and also something to do (drink beer, eat beer nuts) during the inevitable long and awkward silences. You and your future father-in-law won't have to face each other down for very long and most of the conversation can be done while looking into the crowded bar mirror.

I also like the idea of a walk down a busy sidewalk. It's casual and friendly, and keeping moving is always good to mask the tremor in your voice. Plus, as you're out in a crowd, the old man's not going to haul off and belt you if he's so inclined, and, as previously mentioned, there's minimal eye contact.

Another optimal place for the asking is while the two of you are working under the hood of a car. Or when the old boy is showing you his collection of track and field medals from Wheatley High. In any of those situations, you don't have to go eyeball to eyeball and changing the subject is easy. (By the way, never attempt this conversation while you're watching television.)

Chapter 2

Grabbing the Championship Ring

*Nothing in all the world is more dangerous
than sincere ignorance and conscientious stupidity.*
—Martin Luther King, Jr.

(Translation: You're going to need help buying the ring. Get it. Don't throw up a brick.)

Among the many things a man must do to grease the old Conestoga wagon wheels for a successful, smooth, emotionally safe, and sexy ride to the altar, there may be nothing more important than finding an engagement ring that fulfills all your future bride's dreams. Get it wrong and you might spend the first several years of your marriage and considerable amount of cash at places such as Bed, Bath & Beyond and assorted country antique stores atoning for your sins. Get it really wrong and you could derail the whole wagon train.

But wait…wait…wait! Before you drop this book and start racing for the nearest Bud Light sign, please understand this: It is not that hard to get the right ring. In fact, you almost have to try to get it wrong. (And if that's the case, you just might want to consider postponing the proposal for a while.)

First of all, if she's really going to marry you, she loves you, which means that practically any ring you buy with a clear conscience and a loving intent will make her heart soar. All jokes aside, she loves you for you, not for the car you drive or the way your pecs shimmer in the beach sun or, for that matter, how big a diamond you can get her. (If that doesn't immediately smack of the truth, then drop the book and run like your life depends on it—it does.) Plus, although she has been dreaming of that ring since she was old enough to pretend she was walking down the aisle, the ring is not a single ring. There are lots of rings that she will love—and love you for getting one for her. You don't have to find the one ring in the entire universe like it's some kind of holy grail. The moment she sees the ring you have chosen wisely, it will miraculously become the ring she has been envisioning since she was 5 years old. Lots of different rings will fit the bill, and getting it right is not nearly as hard as it might appear.

Also, despite what officious wedding planners try to tell you, always keep in mind that getting married is not rocket science, nor is it fraught with the dangers of buying on margin, turning a double play, or even spending an evening with your boss. Some of the dumbest people in the world successfully buy engagement rings and eventually get married and live as happily ever after as anyone ever has a right to expect.

So, before you check your wallet or your credit card balances, keep in mind the basic rules of ring shopping:

Pre-Game Ground Rules

9 Things Not to Do

1. **Do not enter a jewelry store alone.** Honestly, the only jewels most men know about are the family jewels—and those are the last things you want driving this purchase, even if you thought it would help you score. After a house and a car (and the Harley you'll purchase when you're 39 or 49), this ring may be the most expensive purchase you make in your marriage. So don't go it alone. An unattached male in a jewelry store is a perfect mark for flirtatious sales clerks ("Oh, I wish I had a guy as sweet and generous as you") or fatherly diamond merchants ("Don't be cheap, son...when she gets a load of this eye candy, you'll be made in the shade"). Very dangerous. Go shopping with someone who's not as emotionally involved or vulnerable as you are. And, as an extra precaution, it would be a good idea to leave your credit cards at home when you go diamond viewing for the first time.

2. **Do not think there is a substitute for a diamond.** Not even if it's absolutely exquisite (or so says the cute babe in the tight sweater behind the counter). Not even if it's an emerald. Or a sapphire. Or, heaven forbid, a heart-shaped ruby. And never, ever, ever, ever a cubic zirconium. Ever. EVER. The phrase "Diamonds are forever" is not just an advertising ploy.

3. **Do not trust your own eyes.** All diamonds are shiny and they all look exquisite on the black velvet display or on the elegant finger of the hand model shop clerk stroking your engorged ego. If your fiance herself is not there to handpick the stone, stick rigidly to the facts you are about to learn. Just the facts. Get the best combination (see The Four Cs on page 33) for the prettiest one at the highest price you can afford. And remember that cost is definitely tied to quality.

4. **Do not ask your best friend for his advice.** Unless he's a jeweler, Ollie (or Hoppy or Dave or Rondon) does not know jack about jewelry or diamond rings. He may know everything there is to know about women, and he may tell you that ring buying is brain surgery, but he's definitely not the one to guide you through this operating room.

5. **Do not ask her mother** unless you're sure that she's going to think she's not losing a daughter, but gaining a son. Your future mother-in-law could be a real asset in the ring hunt, but please know this terrain is full of landmines. Be careful. First, she probably doesn't know about the marriage yet, and you'll be ruining the once-in-a-lifetime surprise for her. Second, it's quite possible that your girlfriend might not want her mother to know before she does. And third, when your future mother-in-law selects the Hope diamond and says it's exactly what her daughter has been dreaming about since she was five, you're going to look like a cheapskate when you show up with something more in ordinary mortal price range. (In the interests of full disclosure, I should add that my wife actually did help sons-in-law Jon and Jeffrey find the right rings for our daughters—and everything worked out just fine. Actually, better than fine.

6. **Do not buy the ring from of your cousin Morty, the ex-con, or some random guy on the street.** Fact: No woman wants a hot ring, even if cousin Morty swears on his mother's grave that it once belonged to Princess Brunhilde of Austria. Even if it's drop-dead gorgeous. Even if it's twice the ring you could afford if you were buying one at a jewelry store. I shouldn't have to mention this—this is a no-brainer of profound dimension—don't. Just don't. However, if you're thinking about it, close this book, put it in a bag, and return it to the bookstore for a refund. You may be beyond my help.

7. **Do not give her your former fiance's ring…or your mother's or grandma's ring.** Don't think she won't care if the ring you give her was once intended for a previous fiance or if it's your mother's or your grandmother's—even if it's beautiful and four times the size of the one you can afford. The first (an earlier broken engagement) is simply a universal taboo; giving her that ring will bring you heartache and pain for seven generations. And the second may indeed be a very sweet idea—and save you a lot of cash—but the last person your wife will ever want to be compared to is your mother. (That goes for cooking, too.) Also, there could be some very sticky ownership problems of the family heirloom if the marriage doesn't work out. (See Chapter 8.)

8. **Do not think that because you can't see flaws in the stone with your naked eye that your bionic bride doesn't know that they are there.** She knows. She also knows when you are sleeping. She knows when you're awake. She knows if you've been sly or cheap, so be a mensch for goodness sake.

9. **Do not passively agree to the price the jeweler quotes for the ring.** Remember to bargain. Even after he or she has pulled out the handheld calculator and figured out the special discounted price "just for you." As my Uncle Murray used to say, "Everyone's got a lower price." Especially jewelers. And as my Uncle Mac, used to say, "Don't send his kids to college on your ring."

Now...Just Three Things To Do

The Do's are much simpler than the Don'ts. There are only three reasonable courses of action to obtain the correct holy rock:

1. **Ask your intended what she wants.** Go against your well-developed courtship and mating instincts and try being honest and direct. Propose well (if necessary, using one of the scenarios developed in Chapter 3)—and then tell her that because you want the ring to be perfect, you want her to pick it out. (It will be important at that time to have an obviously plastic substitute bubble gum ring to slip on her finger. Don't give her anything that might make her wonder—even for a second—that it's the real ring. Give her some bauble that will make her laugh and think you're sweet—and so you are.) And then be sure to let your beloved know that you intend to be at her side the entire time to find the ring of her dreams.

   This is a safe and mature and respectful option. And she will love you for wanting to go into a jewelry store with her. However, it is *not* terrifically romantic—and the proposal, as you can imagine, is missing the glittering centerpiece to the whole memorable event.

2. **Ask your mother.** This is almost always a safe and productive route to bling bling happiness—and it did work out very well for my sons Cael and Danny. However, it, too, does have significant drawbacks. First, it's a very good bet that she knows her way around the diamond. Second, it's an even better bet that she has taken better notice than you regarding your girlfriend's taste in jewelry. And third, because you are her prince (and always will be) she will take great care in finding a beautiful ring that will not put you in danger of having your throne repossessed.

   There is one potential pitfall, however, that you should consider before asking your mother to help you pick out a ring. That is, your mother does not really know your girlfriend as well as you think she does—or she thinks she does. In fact, it's more likely that they've both been on their best behaviors throughout the entire courtship and, as a result, haven't been completely honest with each other. So ponder this: Mother has a pear-shaped diamond that girlfriend once said is the most beautiful ring she has ever seen (despite the fact that she's been dreaming of an emerald cut since she was 5 years old). You know where this is going.

3. **Ask her sister—or her best friend—or her mother (if you're really really sure that's a good idea).** Beg if necessary. I believe this is the optimal choice, if it's available. Her sister or her best friend will probably know everything about the ring of your beloved's dreams down to the shape, setting, and the exact number of points she *needs* to feel properly betrothed. They have been discussing it since they were 5 years old…in sandboxes, at MacDonald's, in school buses, during slumber parties, in bars, at bistros, in college classes, and, of course, at every engagement party and wedding they've ever been to. They know. Plus, if you ask nicely and try to seem more inept than you actually are in this area, one of them might even be willing to take you to the jewelry store she's been visiting every other day for the past six years.

Of course, as with all things in life, there is a downside to this option: The sister or best friend may be so excited—or harbor just enough resentment—that she might not be able to keep your romantic intentions a secret. If it's possible, get some juicy gossip on her and then swear her to secrecy.

Just the Facts, Ma'am

Now that you've got the logistics of ring buying under your belt, it's time to learn something about the rock itself. I'm sorry, but you are going to need to acquaint yourself with a glossary of terms before heading out on this quest. You certainly don't have to memorize them (there is no test), but as with looking under the hood of your car with a mechanic, it's best not to seem like an utter fool.

So before you shop, learn the native lingo of the jewelry jungle. Here are some words you'll need to know to decipher what your jeweler is saying to you (probably to try to confuse you):

Baguettes: A stone cut in the form of a narrow rectangle.
Blemish: Not a pimple. It's a flaw on the surface of a diamond, such as a scratch, abrasion, nick, or chip.
Blue-White: This refers to a diamond that glows (fluoresces) blue under ultraviolet light. (I know, who cares?)
Brilliance: White light reflected back from a diamond.
Brilliant: Not brilliance. Brilliant is a round diamond with 58 facets. (See Facet.)
Carat: A unit of weight, equal to 200 milligrams. Generally speaking, the more carats, the more expensive.
Carbon: The raw material of which diamonds are made. Some diamonds will contain tiny pockets of carbon that can be seen as black spots within the stone. Not good.
Cloud: A cluster of small inclusions, or internal flaws, within a diamond. Also, not a good thing.
Crown: The top of a diamond; everything above the girdle. (See Girdle.)
Culet: The bottom facet of a diamond, usually very small. (Check Facet again in case you've already forgotten.)
Dispersion: Colored light reflected from within a diamond; also called "fire."
Eye-Clean: Refers to a diamond that has no inclusions or blemishes visible to the naked eye.
Facet: A polished surface on a diamond. A round, full-cut diamond usually has 58 facets.
Fluorescence: A diamond's reaction to ultraviolet (UV) light, causing the stone to glow in various colors. (Again, who cares?)
Full-Cut: A diamond with 58 or more facets.
Gemologist: A person who has been trained and certified in diamonds and colored stones.
GIA: Gemological Institute of America, an indepedent, non-profit organization that sets and upholds standards for grading diamonds and other precious stones.

(cont'd)

Girdle: The narrow, unpolished band around the widest part of the diamond; the girdle separates the crown and the pavilion of the stone.

Head: (No, not that.) The prongs that hold a diamond in its setting.

Inclusion: A flaw within a diamond, such as a carbon spot or fracture.

Karat: The measure of the purity of gold, 24-karat being pure gold. Jewelry is also made from 18K and 14K gold, which contain added metals for strength.

Laser-Drilled: A diamond that has been treated with a laser to remove carbon spots.

Loupe: A small magnifying glass used to view gemstones.

Off-Make: A poorly proportioned diamond.

Pave: A method of setting diamonds very close together, giving the illusion of one or more larger diamonds.

Pavilion: The bottom of a diamond; everything below the diamond's girdle.

Point: One-hundredth of a carat. A diamond weighing 1 1/2 carats weighs 150 points.

Semi-Mount: A setting that is complete except for the main stone, which will be selected separately.

Single-Cut: A diamond with only 16 or 17 facets.

Sparkle: The liveliness of the light reflecting from a diamond; the sum of the brilliance and the fire (dispersion).

Tiffany: A simple, elegant 2–3 mm ring setting with a head that holds a single diamond. (This is sometimes called a solitaire.)

Okay, now that you've already forgotten the terms, dog-ear the page so that you can refer to it when you get to the next section, which is really important.

Shape

This is the first important stop on the diamond train. Everything follows from this simple piece of information. Using whatever tools are at your disposal, find out *for sure* what shape she wants—and guessing is not allowed. There are only eight possible shapes:

1. Marquise
2. Heart
3. Princess
4. Emerald

5. Oval
6. Radiant
7. Pear
8. Round

That's it. It doesn't matter what you like, it's totally her call. Most engagement rings are round, so that's a bit of a guide, but don't assume that's what she wants.

The Four Cs

Once you know (for sure) what shape she wants, then you need to consider the Four Cs: Cut, Clarity, Color, and Carat.

Cut

First, cut is not shape. A stone's cut (sometimes called the "make") refers to the number, placement, and shape of the "facets" (flat, polished planes) that create a finished diamond. Nothing is more critical to a diamond's sparkle and fire than the quality of its cut, so this is very important. And a diamond must, must, must sparkle.

Several grading systems exist. The Gemological Institute of America ranks cuts from Class I (ideal) to Class IV (poor). Ultimately, however, your eye will be the final judge. I suggest you hold the diamond with tweezers and examine it straight on, as if it were in a setting, to see if it twinkles with a seamless sparkle and rainbow of colors. (Ask to see a range of makes to see the differences—they are easily apparent and very important.) A stone that appears dull or dark at the center probably suffers from a bad cut job.

Color

Although diamonds actually come in some startling shades of blue, red, pink, amber, orange, and canary yellow, the diamonds you'll probably want to be looking at—and will be able to afford—will range from white to yellow. When it comes to color, less is more. All you really need to know is that *the whiter the diamond, the better*: More light will pass through it and be reflected as sparkle. Simple as that.

Following are the GIA color grades:

GIA Color Grades

D, E, F: Colorless (white).
G, H, I: Nearly colorless.
J, K, L: Slightly yellow.
M, N, O: Light yellow.
P, Q, R, S, T, U, V, W, X: Darker yellow.
Z: "Fancy" colors.

Bottom line, the professionals advice from *Diamonds.com*, my local jeweler Bill Luedeke, and the ultimate diamond expert, my wife, all agree: Get an H or an I. Once mounted, it'll look just as good as the higher grades, and you'll still have enough money left over to go on a honeymoon.

Clarity

The clarity of a diamond depends on how clear or "clean" the diamond is, that is, how free of imperfections on the outside (blemishes) and inside (inclusions) of the stone when viewed with the naked eye and with a loupe (10X magnifying glass). Blemishes include chips, scratches, fractures, or polishing mistakes; inclusions consist of spots and "feathers" (internal cracks). Remember: Diamonds are created naturally, so slight inclusions are very common.

The following is a list of the GIA clarity grades:

GIA Clarity Grades

Fl = flawless.

> Free from inclusions and blemishes when viewed under 10X magnification. Extremely rare and expensive.

IF = internally flawless.

> Free from inclusions; may have slight blemishes when viewed under 10X magnification. Also very rare and expensive.

VVS1, VVS2 = very, very slightly included.

> Has minute inclusions or blemishes the size of a pinpoint when viewed under 10X magnification. Rare and expensive.

VS1, VS2 = very slightly included.

> Has inclusions or blemishes smaller than a grain of salt when viewed under 10X magnification. High quality.

SI1, SI2 = slightly included.

> Has inclusions or blemishes larger than a grain of salt when viewed under 10X magnification. Almost all SI1 diamonds are "eye-clean," which means the flaws can't be seen with the naked eye, and are considered good quality. SI2 stones may have imperfections visible to the naked eye. Borderline.

I1, I2, I3 = imperfect.

> Has inclusions and blemishes visible to the naked eye that make the diamond look cloudy and lifeless. Definitely **not recommended** for the love of your life!

My experts' advice? Shoot for a SI1 to VS1 stone. (And one final suggestion: If you opt for a low clarity grade, the triangular or kite-shaped facets of a round, brilliant-cut stone hide flaws better than the rectangular facets of an emerald or step-cut stone.)

Carat

A carat is a unit of weight (not to be confused with karat, which indicates gold's purity). Carat is derived from the word carob, the bean that's often used as a chocolate substitute. Carob trees grow in the Mediterranean region; in ancient times, a diamond of one carat...okay, I can see your eyes rolling...so let's go on: Diamond weights are also referred to in points. One carat equals 100 points, so a 75-point diamond would weigh 3/4 carat.

For pricing information based on carat size and clarity, turn to the Appendix.

Chapter 3

The Playbook

Eight Fill-in-the-Blank Proposal Scripts
(It's like Mad Libs, but you don't need to know the difference between verbs and adverbs.)

*K*eep the proposal short and sweet and make it sound sincere. It should be. You want her, you need her, you love her...but if you're like hundreds of thousands of your tongue-tied brethren, you simply do not know what to say to convince her that you alone will be the man of her dreams—forever.

For those of you who read *Cyrano de Bergerac* (or saw *Roxanne* or watched the Fox sideshow about marrying a millionaire), you already know the questionable benefits and disastrous pitfalls of speaking someone else's words of love. Trust me, you can get yourself in a powerful load of trouble if she even thinks momentarily that you're being insincere.

However, if you have also had the opportunity of seeing your friends (or yourself, for that matter) choking on lame pickup lines or just plain old choking when it comes to asking out a girl, you must also be aware that there is only humiliation and defeat awaiting any man who doesn't know exactly what he's going to say when it's crunch time at center courtship.

Keep in mind, this phase of the courtship is probably not a deal maker or breaker—unless you're fool enough to ask someone you don't know well enough to marry you (and she's a bigger fool than you by actually considering it). At best, premature proposers look like they have little impulse control and perhaps can't be trusted to be anybody's trusted husband. At worst, they look desperate, like stalkers in training. So make sure you know your intended—and her intentions—very well before trying out one of these scripts.

And please know this: Your girlfriend—like most women—is often a step ahead of you on the marriage wheel, so odds are that she has had some intuition in the days or weeks ahead about when you're going to propose. And even if she doesn't have the date pegged exactly, she already knows what she is going to say when you finally (finally!) get around to saying it.

That said, I know this whole process is powerfully daunting. It's opening up drivers tests, SAT results, college acceptance letters, MCATs, and medical tests, all rolled in one. In many ways it feels as if your whole future depends on how she responds to your well-considered proposal—and, let's be honest, in many ways it is.

It was daunting enough that Sir Edmund Hillary, the first Westerner to reach the summit of Mount Everest and arguably one of the bravest men who ever lived, was so tongue-tied that his mother-in-law had to pop the question for him. That is not a recommended option, but you should know that it worked.

According to psychotherapist and marital counselor Dr. Marj Steinfeld, "Rule number one is that you don't want to ask her at an inappropriate time." Don't pop the question while her mouth is full of food or when she's racing to get ready for a party or online or over your cell phones or when she's on the pot. Find the right time and the right place. Don't rush it.

Keep in mind, too, that simply being nervous is not a flaw during this phase of the courtship. As Dr. Steinfeld says, "Most women seek out strong and decisive men, but they also don't want to marry some arrogant narcissist who merely assumes they're going to say yes. They definitely want to know that their future husbands need them, too." Translation: Most women think nervousness is cute in men asking for their hands in matrimony.

But don't be too cute.

- Don't memorize your speech. It sounds phony. (If you're really nervous and you botch the memorization part, though, you can cross over into cute. However, this is not something you can plan.)
- Don't read the proposal (unless you're specifically using the Grand Gesture see page 42).
- Don't have the TV on while you're doing it. I hope I don't need to explain this.

- ☞ Don't have a crowd of family or friends around you waiting to serve up high fives when the deed is done. Except for those who love the Grand Gesture, the marriage proposal is an intimate moment and, as such, is best done alone.
- ☞ Don't go on and on. It's one sign of nervousness (or arrogance) that quickly loses its charm.
- ☞ Don't call her a girl or "the best thing" in your life. You're asking a woman to marry you and perhaps even be the mother of your children. She's not a thing.
- ☞ After you have asked your sweetheart for her hand, don't make plans for that evening that do not include her. I shouldn't have to mention this, but you'd be surprised how many guys go out with "the boys" soon after brushing the dirt from their knees.

So, here they are. Above all, keep the proposal short and sweet—two minutes or less total from the "I have a question to ask you..." to the final slipping the ring on her finger. (Review Chapter 2.) Take her hand gently and, as your mom always told you, look her directly in the eye, take a deep breath...and then deliver one of the following scripts for a predictably successful and memorable moment.

They are listed in order of effectiveness from least to most. (Note: I'd be very very wary of the least—and, in fact, I'd only advise using number 7 or 8, but you know yourself and your sweetie better than I do.)

I. Thematic

If your relationship was initiated on or has been built around a theme such as hiking, dancing, sailing, Jeopardy, PETA activism, the Kennedy assassination, whatever...you might want to try this format. What follows are two examples of theme-driven scenarios that you can easily modify for your own special interests. You'll note that they are very similar and similarly very short—and the really important part of each one is the location. As you might imagine, theme proposals are best enacted in the environment around which the original connection was made.

The downside is that no matter how you do it, the presentation will sound a little rehearsed or artificial—and perhaps downright corny. The upside, however, is that you'll be acknowledging something that's very important to her and also be suggesting that you want to bring your shared passion to a new level. Plus, corniness, like nervousness, is never to be underestimated as an appealing aspect of successful courtship.

1. The Hiker. Location: Off the side of a quiet and beautiful trail (preferably one with a view) on a gorgeous day. WARNING: Do not attempt this one in bad weather:

   (Insert name), I love you with all my heart and soul. If I had one wish in life it would be for you to walk the trail of life with me forever. Take the ring out of your backpack (and, if necessary, wipe the granola bits off the box)...*Will you make me the happiest hiker in the world and be my bride?*

2. The Sailor. Location: On a beautiful, quiet, and languid lake or river on a gorgeous day. As above, don't attempt this in bad weather:

   (Insert name), I love you with all my heart. I want you to know that I'd like nothing more than for you to sail down the river of life with me. Take the ring out of your windbreaker pocket (and wipe the droplets of water off the box)...*Please make me the happiest mate on the water and say you'll marry me.*

II. The Silent Persuader

The silent persuader is for the strong, silent type—or at least the silent type. It's all about action and no talk...a terrific way for those who are uncomfortable expressing their emotions to let their thoughtful actions speak louder than their words.

This one might work well for the tongue-tied—or the supremely confident—or if you're simply too busy to devote that much time to a big theatrical production. (In the latter case, you might want to reconsider the merger and examine the consequences of what might be termed a hostile takeover.) The upside is that you don't look like a fool. The downside is that you're not putting anything on the line—and, although you should be, you may not even be there.

Major Warning

Never hide the ring in food that she's going to eat. Although we see this scene played out often enough on television sitcoms, it is not only potentially lethal, it's not funny. And it's disgusting to watch someone yanking what she thinks is a tooth or a piece of bone out of her mouth. Plus, there's always the potential for an expensive root canal following a cracked tooth.

Try these instead—and remember, you need to be present or at least nearby to see her joy and accept her hugs and kisses (and maybe even a few tears):

1. The Debonair: Place a black or blue velvet ring box on the cozy restaurant table while she's visiting the rest room—or on her desk at work when she's out to lunch. The box should be opened with lights focused on the glittering diamond. Right next to it you should place a beautiful note in calligraphic script (never typed, never written in pencil) that says:

   Will you marry me? I love you with all my heart, (and don't forget to insert her name).

2. The Sweetheart: With flowers (or chocolates) attached and delivered by reliable courier to her door at work or home. Make sure the ring box is wrapped in metallic paper with a bow—or at least tightly shut. In this scenario, you might want to be hiding in the bushes or out in the hall—and you must make your entrance within 10 seconds of her opening the ring box and reading the proposal. (And make sure that you don't get arrested as a Peeping Tom or stalker.)

3. Teacher's Pet: Attached to the collar of her beloved dog or cat. One caveat: Be absolutely sure that the animal comes when called.

4. Old Blue Eyes: The singing telegram proposal. (Not a male stripper. And definitely not a female stripper.)

III. The Grand Silent Gesture: Big Signs

This "script" is perfect for the tongue-tied or the naturally preposterous. (Because these proposals are generally so public, you need to be doubly sure that she's going to say yes—and that she'll think you're wonderful for asking in this manner. If you embarrass her or make her feel trapped, you'll never ever again get another chance.)

Although each company or office has different policies regarding public displays, to get the ball rolling you should phone or e-mail the public relations department of the organization. In most cases they will be glad to help you (and will be pleased to get some publicity for their company along the way).

Keep in mind that these ideas generally take a lot of preparation and often a lot of money, but that should be the only complicated part of the whole event. Everything else needs to be kept very simple. Above all, don't make the actual question dependent on too many variables. Nothing more than: (*Her name**), *I LOVE you. Will you marry me?* (*Your name**) (*Names are especially important to this one.)

1. The Commuter: On a billboard she passes every day on her way to work.
2. The Bush Pilot: On an ad trailing off the back of a small plane. Be sure to instruct the pilot to make several passes. Be sure to have the note start with her name. Be sure to be there. Be sure to have a rain date.
3. The Fan: Take her to a ball game and pay an exorbitant fee to pop the question on the scoreboard. Keep in mind that the television cameras will be focused on you and your sweetie during the whole scene—and thereafter. Don't be caught picking your nose or worse on national TV. And, above all, you must be supremely confident that she will say yes—and that she won't be as mortified as you would at being the center of such outlandish attention.
4. The Old College Try: Another ball game scenario: I've seen this one arranged at college football games where placards are often part of the spectators' scene. As you

might imagine, this one is very difficult to set up, but it will make a stunning spectacle. You really need to know someone at the boosters office at the college. Above all, make sure she's in the stands when the message is flashed—there are no do-overs for this one.
5. The Fake Left and Go Right: Another placard scenario. This one is much more easily controlled than the one that takes place in a stadium, but is far smaller in scope. If she's a teacher, as in the Robert DeNiro movie *Meet the Parents,* have 10 reliable kids each hold up a piece of construction paper with one word of the proposal when she enters a classroom—or walks outside for recess. To accomplish this, you must get the okay from the principal (or the cops may arrest you for trespassing on school property and harassing children). If she's not a teacher, pay 10 neighborhood kids $5 apiece to hold up the signs when you walk by the park at the appointed time. If they run off with the money and the construction paper, give it up and ask her yourself.
6. The Workaholic: On the screen saver at work. This is a nice touch for the tech-savvy. Be sure to add a note in small letters at the bottom of the screen: "Look in the top drawer of your desk." Be sure to have the ring in the desk. Be sure to be there in the shadows—or show up in an IM right away.

IV. The Sales Pitch

In this scenario you are trying to convince your coy or unconvinced beloved that you are the one—or at least that you are better than all the others. Use this only if you're really not sure that she's going to say yes. You might end up looking like you're trying too hard, the only unforgivable sin identified so far in the 21st century:

(Her name), in the short/long time I've known you, I've come to see that you are a very, very special person. (Take her hand and look her in the eyes.) *First, I want you to know that I love you with all my heart. That's the most important thing of all. But I also don't believe that unbounded love is enough for me (or any man) to ask someone as special as you for her hand in marriage.*

(Note: If she raises her eyebrows at this point and looks surprised, say something along the lines of, *"Yes, it is the greatest desire in my life right now for you to be my bride."* If she then rolls her eyes or glances furtively at the exit, excuse yourself and keep running until you get to a pawnshop. However, if she smiles, keep going....)

(Name), I want you to know that I promise:

Now, list your qualities according to her priority of needs (I'd choose three or four *max*):

1. *To give my life for you.*
2. *To climb the highest mountain, swim the deepest sea, to make you happy.*
3. *Respect your freedom to be exactly who you are and whoever you wish to be.*
4. *Support your dreams and your career in any way I can.*
5. *Be the best man I can be for you.*
6. *Be the best father I can be.* (Be careful here. Make sure she's on the same page.)
7. *Will always and ever be true to her.* (Never say the word cheat.)
8. *Laugh with you through everything we face together.*
9. *Be your friend and partner in all we do.*
10. *Work day and night to allow you to live as a queen.*

Then (finally):

I promise, (insert name again), all that and more, if you'll make me the happiest man in the universe and be my bride. (Don't say wife—it sounds too old and settled.)

V. The New Age Spiritual Empowerment Scenario

We are living through the Self-Help Era. You'd be hard-pressed to find anyone in this country who has not been to some form of counseling, listened to Oprah, or read something with a title that begins "10 Steps to...."

With that in mind, this type of proposal can be a stunning tool to convince your beloved that you are not only good looking, but have the New Age sensitivity and sophistication to support her quest to be who she really is. Here are the seven words that must show up in this kind of proposal:

1. Journey.
2. Share.
3. Fulfill(ing).
4. Learn.
5. Respect.
6. Love.
7. Grow.

They are the seven doors to domestic bliss. In creating your own proposal, as you experiment mixing and matching the key words or sound bytes, try something like this (and remember that eye contact is as importantas ever):

(*Her name*), *over the past weeks/months/years we've shared so much together. It's not only been the most* _____ *time of my life, but I've grown so much as I've learned about myself and life itself through you. I hope I've given you as much as you've given me on your own journey.*

Take her hand.

(*Repeat her name*), *I love you. I* _____ *who you are. I* _____ *what you do. Would you do me the honor of joining me in bringing our relationship to the next level of commitment?*

Reveal the ring.

VI. The Literary Proposal

This type of scenario might work well with English teachers, graduate students, younger writers (never older ones), editorial assistants, interns (not senior editors), librarians of all ages, and assorted others who find the sight of a rolled book bulging out of the buttocks pocket of a male's jeans oddly stirring.

The literary proposal has the remarkable benefit of script and props. That is, you're not alone out there on the stage. You're allowed to read from a book or a piece of paper folded 16 times and pulled out of your pocket. Plus, there is almost no way for you to forget or stumble over your lines.

Two caveats: First, be sure you can pronounce all the words, and, second, have a pretty good idea what the poet is actually trying to say.

Always start with something along these lines:

(*Her Name*), *I want you to know that I love you so much that I don't have the words to express it myself.* (If she looks annoyed or disturbed, you might want to wait for another time or place. However, if she smiles demurely or wells up or says simply, "I love you, too," then take her hand.) *So I found this by (name of author), who comes as close as any human can to saying what is in my heart:*

Choose only one (this is not a lecture or a seminar):

1. "How Do I Love Thee?" by Elizabeth Barret Browning (*Immortal Poems of the English Language*, Williams, Ed., Washington Square Press, 1952). This, of course, is the romantic poem of all time. It's corny, way overused, and dated...but it works:

How Do I Love Thee?

How do I love thee? Let me count the ways.
I love thee to the breadth and depth and height
My soul can reach, when feeling out of sight
For the ends of Being and ideal Grace.
I love thee to the level of everyday's
Most quiet need, by sun and candle-light.
I love thee freely as men strive for Right;
I love thee purely, as they turn from Praise.
I love thee with the passion put to use
In my old griefs, and with my childhood's faith.
I love thee with a love I seemed to lose
With my lost saints—I love thee with the breath,
Smiles, tears, of all my life!—and, if God choose,
I shall but love thee better after death.

2. "Shall I Compare Thee" by William Shakespeare (*The Complete Sonnets and Poems by William Shakespeare*, Oxford University Press, 2002). As in number one, this poem is dated, possible corny, and probably much overused by suitors in all ages. Yet Bill himself is as golden as he was back in the 16th and 17th centuries. You can't go wrong with a poem by Shakespeare—just be sure that you've read it first and know how to say all the words.

Shall I Compare Thee

Shall I compare thee to a summer's day?
Thou art more lovely and temperate:
Rough winds do shake the darling buds of May,
And Summer's lease hath all too short a date:
Sometime too hot the eye of heaven shines,
And often is his gold complexion dimm'd;
And every fair from fair sometimes declines,
By chance or nature's changing course untrimm'd.

By the eternal Summer shall not fade
Nor lose possession of that fair thou ow'st;
Nor shall Death brag thou wander'st in his shade,
When in eternal lines to time thou grow'st:
So long as men can breathe, or eyes can see,
So long lives this, and this gives life to thee.

3. "The Outlet" or "Wild Nights" by Emily Dickinson (*The Complete Poems of Emily Dickenson*, Back Bay Books, 1976)—or almost any poem by the great romantic recluse that isn't somber or full of death images. She will help you convince the most reluctant of lovers, if only just by showing her that you know Dickinson well enough to speak one of her poems without laughing.

The Outlet

My river runs to thee:
Blue sea, wilt thou welcome me?
My river waits reply.
Oh sea, look graciously!
I'll fetch thee brooks
From spotted nooks,—
Say, sea,
Take me!

Wild Nights

Wild nights! Wild nights!
Were I with thee,
Wild nights should be
Our luxury.

Futile the winds
To a heart in port,
Done with the compass,
Done with the chart.

Rowing in Eden!
Ah! The sea!
Might I but moor
To-night in thee!

4. Check out "For Love" by Robert Creeley (*For Love: Poems 1950-1960*, Scribners, 1962). Simply written in conversational style, the elusive themes and meanings in this poem have a quiet and melancholy air, but the final two lines are like the sweetest kiss you could bring to her lips. (She should be an English major if you're going to attempt this one.)

5. I'm also going to suggest looking at "For Tess" by Raymond Carver (*All of Us*, Knopf, 1998). As with the Creeley poem, this is simple and conversational, but here there is tenderness where there was melancholy in "for Love." He is grateful for the quiet joy she brings to his life. This one is guaranteed to be magical.

6. Another suggestion is "It Was When" by Gary Snyder (*Regarding Wave*, New Directions, 1979). This is for the post-hippie, alternative—or wanna-be alternative—types. It's full of nature and peace and good karma and stuff.

7. Any number of poems by Sharon Olds. Careful here, though: Olds is a very sensual artist and the sexual references in her love poems will either be terribly stirring to your lover or will kill the pure mood. Check out "The Gold Cell" (*The Gold Cell*, Knopf, 1987) and see what you think.

VII. Sweet and Simple

The simplest things in our lives are often the best. This simple proposal is not artificial or a scene or larger than life. Its success rests on its lack of pretension and its utter sincerity. It is you unplugged. And all you need to do is find a quiet and pretty place, get down on your knee (yes), take her hand gently and, again, as your mom always told you, look her directly in the eye...and say the following:

I love you with all my heart, (insert name), and I would like nothing more than to share the rest of my life with you. Will you make me the happiest man in the world and marry me?

That's it. It's a doozy (and hard to mess up). Make sure you have the ring ready when she wells up and hugs the breath out of you.

VIII. The Utterly Romantic

Well, I suppose this is the big one. Don't use it unless you're really a romantic at heart. (It'll come back to haunt you later on as a form of false advertising.) As with the Sweet and Simple, it needs to be as brief as a kiss and as flowery as the dozen roses you bring along with it. As with the New Age Spiritual Empowerment scenario, there is a checklist of words you might want to use:

1. Adore.
2. Heart.
3. Breath.
4. Eternity or Eternal (or both).
5. Love.

My Darling,

(Note: Use this form of address—or others similar to it such as "My Love" or "Sweetheart"—only if she's heard you speak those word before. If not, her name will do. You don't want to sound like a phony.)

I adored you from afar before I knew you. And I was breathless the first time our lips touched (give date and place, but only if you're absolutely sure you're right). *But nothing compares to love that has grown in my heart and soul since we've been together as one. Please make me the happiest man in the world and allow me the pleasure of devoting my life to you.*

Get down on your knee and take out the ring.

(Insert her full name here), will you marry me?

And when she says yes, say this as you slide the ring on her finger:

This is only a symbol of the eternal circle of love I hold in my heart for you. I will adore you forever and ever.

And then do just that.

Chapter 4

The Real World of Engagement Stories

I teach at an unusual college, one that offers credit for one's life experiences. At Empire State College, the SUNY "college without walls," we value what people have learned by doing. Which is the way that many men come to understand the world.

This is why I am including these—and other—firsthand testimonials from men and women who walked the walk before you. They're not written by experts or counselors with a jumble of letters after their name—they're just regular folks who have a tale or two to tell. Some of these people are funny, some are sad, some are touching, but all of them, in just telling their stories without trying to teach you anything, may be more instructive than the detailed instructions you'll find elsewhere in this book.

I'll start with me in the spring of 1968, a New York suburban Jew recently be-ringed to the lovely Episcopalian Patti Henderson who grew up in New Orleans. I'll then move on to some others who were kind enough to share their tales of woo and woe.

Meeting My In-Laws

I knew immediately upon stepping out of the plane into the thick hot Louisiana air that I was a fish out of water—or, more appropriately, because fish could probably live in the humid atmosphere of the delta, I was simply out of my element, a wooly panting mutt whose paws get stuck in a swampy muck every time he tries to take a step.

I was dizzy. I was sweaty. I was close to an out of body experience. Actually, I was in Louisiana to meet Patti's mother and father—

and grandmothers and aunts and uncles and cousins and friends and ex-boyfriends—a daunting task for an aggressively shy beatnik poet whose social graces might best be called a little stunted.

And soon enough I was failing miserably at the task of winning over my new family. Although Patti's mother, Nancy, loved me immediately for the very thing I knew in my bones was necessary to hide from my new family—I wrote poetry—my tongue grew swollen when I tried to talk with cousin Bobby or Uncle Bruce and his wife Red. My ears filled with swamp water when I tried to understand the lilting voices of Patti's friends, Clydia, Kingsley, Lettice, and Amalie. I squirmed and sweat like a malaria patient while we had afternoon tea in her grandmother's parlor. My long hair frizzed into an Afro of continental proportions. And the hot shrimp creole her mother prepared felt like burning tar in my matzoh ball mouth.

Then I met her father. An inveterate angler, he had been fishing on the Gulf when I had arrived, so Nancy arranged an extended family picnic at Lake Ponchatrain where he would meet us on his way home. Charles Crawford Henderson arrived in a grayish Chevy wagon and strode right across the grass in my direction, arms swinging, face lined and burnt—a vision of Southern manhood—right hand extended. My hand looked like a dead whitefish in his reddish brown paw.

His very first words to me were, "So, do you fish?"

If it was physically possible to grow paler than I already was, I'm certain I blanched. "Well, yes, no, I mean I've been fishing, but, y'know, I'm not really...."

He looked angry. "Well, do you hunt?"

"Ummm, no...."

Now he looked confused. My throat was clogged, my armpits a dismal swamp, my mind a flooding bayou. Finally I uttered the only thing that made it through the muck: "Patti and I rode horses over at Audubon Park today."

"Oh," he lit up, "you ride horses?"

"Well," I sank quickly in the deep muck. "No, not really, it was my first time."

He shook his head and looked haplessly over at Uncle Bruce, who turned away speechless, then cousin Bobby, who looked down at his sneakers with a smirk. "Well, let's see," the old man said about to make a list with his fingers, "you don't fish, you don't hunt, you don't ride horses. Just what do you do, son?"

While looking for a tree to back up against in case I fainted—or got attacked—I scurried around behind my glazing eyes desperately searching for some manly conversation to please the old man. A fourth-year college sophomore didn't seem quite impressive enough. A former high school athlete who hadn't run across a highway in at least three years didn't seem to be the key. A bourbon drinker might have been a possibility, but it was too risky.

My mouth opened but nothing came out. It seemed like the whole extended family, extending back several generations, was leaning in my direction, waiting for my answer. Patti's father had his hands on his hips, waiting. Patti's eyes were as wide as a Raggedy Ann doll's as I stood there drowning in my own juices.

Then from behind, right over my left shoulder like a fairy godmother, came Patti's mother's soft southern drawl, "Why! He's a poet, Charles."

I vaguely remember my new father-in-law's eyes rolling back into his manly head. The groan I imagine he suppressed might have created a tidal wave on the lake. I don't remember anything after that. But we're still married.

The Great Plans of Mice and Boys

—Cael Lewis, sales and marketing, Saugerties, N.Y.

(As told in part by his disbelieving father with gaps filled in by his smirking sister, Nancy).

As I understand it, the actual life-altering decision came between halves of an ACC basketball game, Corona in hand. I imagine Dick Vitale cheering himself into instant muteness, random camera shots of smiling 35-year-olds with beers in hand flashing silently across the TV screen.

It was definitely time to make a move. Time to stop running the give and go. No more prowling nights at the Cat's Cradle in Chapel Hill, no more parading around on his laurels as butt-quarters champ of Sigma Pi at Florida State (FSU), no more second thoughts about Trish the Dish or hometown cutie Niki George. He would suck it up and ask the beautiful and devoted Melissa to marry him.

Now what? (As if there was anything else to do....)

As an economics major at FSU with some experience in marketing, he understood the importance of location. He also knew he had to get a ring. That was it.

Location was a virtual no-brainer: the family's small beach cottage on Hatteras Island, North Carolina, was not only romantically empty in April, but it also had cable.

The diamond ring thing, though, had him stumped. (Having grown up with four sisters, Cael knew there was a right diamond ring, he just had no idea what "right" could possibly mean in this particular circumstance.) As you might imagine, his good friends Oliver, Jimmy, and Sherm were no help at all. Nor was his backup man, me. So Cael was, in the already overused vernacular of 1995, clueless.

But not resourceless. He called his mother in upstate New York and pleaded hapless confusion. As many boys discover early on, utter bewilderment in the presence of a female is a simple and elegant solution to a lot of problems.

And so it was no problem convincing his mother that it was her maternal duty to save her 25-year-old boy from a lifetime of loneliness by shopping around for a diamond ring impressive enough to persuade Melissa not to have second thoughts of her own.

He gave Patti an approximate budget, stroked her maternal ego by saying he absolutely trusted her elegant taste, and was just about to say goodbye when he slipped in that he needed the ring in two weeks. He hung up before she was able to pick herself up off the floor.

Needless to say, Cael was rather satisfied with himself. He had come to a powerfully transforming decision. He had picked out a convenient date (two weeks) and appropriate location (the beach on Hatteras). And he had practically bought a ring.

He even had the foresight to consult the sports section of the Raleigh *News & Record* to find out when the Final Four games would be held (that weekend), and then choreographed in his mind the right location to pop the question (just over the dunes) and the precise time to get down on his knee (sunset), which would give them enough time to share the intimacies of the moment...and then go out for a romantic dinner...and then share the intimacies of the whole evening. And the next day, while Melissa would spend the afternoon calling everyone she knew in the Western Hemisphere, he'd be free to watch the games. It was perfection—Jordan in motion.

Unfortunately, Cael didn't count on any of the seemingly insignificant things that muck up all well-designed plays, such as getting a late start from Chapel Hill on Friday afternoon, the massive traffic jam on I-40 around Raleigh, Melissa's infuriating day at work and consequent black mood, or even that all the beach restaurants were still closed for the season.

Or the salient fact that the date he chose to propose might cause a problem or two.

Plus, how was he to know that the jeweler wouldn't have *the* ring just sitting there in his shop—and that there was just no way in hell that anyone (not even his mother) would be able to beam it to North Carolina in time to slip it on his future bride's finger whilst he was on his sandy knee.

Thus, arriving ringless on the Outer Banks just as the orange sun was about to drown itself in Pamlico Sound, Cael practically had to drag Melissa out to the beach where upon being asked—empty-handedly—for her hand in Holy Matrimony, Melissa took a small step backward, smirked and wondered aloud if it was an April Fool's joke.

Yes, it was April Fool's Day.

Wounded, Cael assured her he was not joking.

She persisted.

He insisted.

And twice more assured that he was being sincere, Melissa finally uttered the eternal "Yes!" (still wondering if it was a prank). Then they kissed and went out for pizza.

It was obviously not quite the vision of romantic perfection that either of them had conjured up. Nevertheless, Cael and Melissa were engaged and they would have a good story to tell their kids some day. She was happy. And he was happy—and, short of signing for the ring and slipping it on his fiance's empty finger when it arrived by FedEx two weeks late, Cael naturally assumed he was finished with his part of the deal. All that was left was to go along with Oliver and the rest of his friends for a bachelor party that I'm glad I wasn't invited to.

Meeting the Minister

—Evan Selinske, Nanuet, N.Y.

My lovely bride-to-be and I were a little nervous about our first meeting with my parent's minister, who was to marry us in a joint ceremony with the local monsignor. The minister had a reputation for being a stern, no-nonsense type who had as little patience for frivolous thinking as the thinkers themselves.

Just a moment after we had settled into our chairs, the subject of the reception came up, followed by a little small talk about centerpieces and such, the minister's eyes growing darker and darker by the sentence. But then, my fiance cut it short by saying, "Well, of course everyone gets excited about the reception, but really, the day is all about the ceremony."

The minister's eyes lit up. We relaxed. The meeting went great. And, as I thought about it later, my wife was right. The party was a lot of fun, but nothing else could ever compare to the sight of her coming down the aisle, looking at me all the way.

A Series of Close Calls

—Erin Culbreth, political consultant, Raleigh, N.C.

Sometimes it seems as if life is a series of close calls. My fiance's version of our engagement story is a case in point.

First, Tom was sitting outside the jewelry store getting ready to pick up my beautiful engagement ring. I called him, wondering where he was. Ever the quick thinker, he paused and blurted out, "I'm at the grocery store." (It didn't occur to me to ask why he was at the grocery store at 3 p.m. on a Wednesday.) Almost caught.

Then there was the afternoon he was planning to propose in a romantic hotel in Charleston, South Carolina. Everything was all set, but the poor man had trouble getting the ring out of his "hiding place," which consisted of a velvet bag, in an envelope that was taped, then folded into another envelope, then put into a manila envelope that was sealed with mailing tape and stapled. (FYI: Tom is a lawyer.)

He asked me to go down to the hotel lobby to get a paper to buy some time. Completely unaware of what was about to happen, I strolled down three flights, picked up a paper, walked back up, turned the key and found the door dead bolted before I walked in on him tearing apart all the multi-layered packing! Of course, he had no choice but to let me in the room, but he opened the door and sprinted into the bathroom with the mysterious envelope. Almost caught again.

Then that evening after our engagement we were at the rooftop bar celebrating. I was sitting at a table while he was waiting to get us drinks. A charming French man approached me, striking up a flirtatious conversation. I pointed at Tom, my left hand glistening from the ring, and said my fiance was at the bar getting us drinks. The lovely man kissed my hand and offered his congratulations. Of course, I told Tom he was lucky that he had proposed earlier that day or I could have had a romantic European in hot pursuit! Now almost lost.

Today when I glance down at the beautiful ring, I'm reminded of all the close calls in Charleston—and how, the day after we returned from our romantic weekend, we learned that the jewelry store where Tom bought the ring had been robbed!

A Close Shave

—Erik McCarron, happy family guy, Atlanta, G.A.

My wife's family lives in Germany. The first time that I met them was the week before the wedding, when they traveled to Atlanta with some close family friends to spend quality time with us before our nuptials. My future father- and mother-in-law stayed in our house, which is an adorable but tiny two bedroom, one bath bungalow.

The week was wonderful with fabulous dinners, cookouts, and parties; and I enjoyed every second of getting to know my new family.

However, two days before May 23 (our wedding day), with my brother-in-law, his girlfriend, my mother- and father-in-law, Ceri, and I crowded into our little bungalow, the place quickly filled with the thick electric danger that can only exist when people who know each other the best are in close proximity for too long a period of time, mixed with much alcohol and a serious lack of sleep.

In order to escape for a few moments, I sneaked into the bathroom to shave and trim my hair before we left to see some Atlanta tourist attractions. I was wearing my hair a respectable 3/4 inch above my scalp that I maintained myself with an electric trimmer, a tool that I consider to be slightly more classy than a Flowbee. This hairstyle suited me starting from the time that I realized that the majority of my hair was missing from the top of my head and saved me a bundle on hairdresser bills.

As I finished up, my future wife snuck into the bathroom to evade the same oppressive charge from which I was hiding. She looked at the side of my head and noticed that I had missed a few stray hairs. Being the helpful person that she is, she picked up the trimmer, pressed it against my scalp, and moved it around my ear. What she failed to observe was that I had removed the guard that kept it 3/4 inch long.

She began to laugh hysterically as I looked down at the pile of hair by my feet and then back up to the lawnmower track of missing hair around my ear. She kept repeating that she was so sorry, but the impact was lost amid the shrill pitch of her giggles. I tried the same thing on the other side of my head to effect a sort of retro new wave look, but the result made me look tonsured. Because entering into a life of celibacy was the last thing on my mind two days before my wedding, I had no choice but to take it all off.

Needless to say, our relationship was solid enough to survive this little debacle. As a result, we have the joy of looking at our wedding pictures together, and giggling at the distinguished gentleman with a neatly trimmed goatee and gleaming white scalp.

It Was All on the House

—Jim Russek, advertising executive, Pound Ridge, N.Y.

When we showed her dad the antique engagement ring, he told us we should plan the wedding. Not him. At 65 years old he was still recovering from his own wedding the year before. To his third wife. However, he pledged $25,000 for a wedding.

We got home that night and joked how we should just take the money and buy a house. I was 37. She was 28. We were partied out, and this was her second wedding anyway—the triumph of hope over experience? But when someone offers you $25,000 to throw a wedding, you throw a wedding, right?

We made lists. If you go deep—second cousins— you're at more than 100 people before anybody you really want to share this day with gets invited. We got the list down to 125 accepting there would be blood relatives who would never speak to us again.

When you audition wedding mills, they feed you—free. We went to lofts in SoHo, five-star hotels, and private clubs. The party guy at the St. Regis was the son of the ex-governor of New York. We eventually picked the National Arts Club. They have a magnificent stained glass cupola over the bar and a lovely painting of Dwight D. Eisenhower before the stroke. I invited my future father-in-law and his newish wife to visit the club with us and get their blessing. He really liked the Eisenhower portrait. After our free dinner, however, he told us we were crazy to throw a wedding. "With $25,000 you could buy a house!"

We cancelled the National Arts Club, got married on her dad's lawn in front of parents, siblings, and eight friends. And no joke, we bought a house.

Into the Wind

—Jeffrey Trapani, law student, Jamaica Plain, Mass.

On the Outer Banks, you are either heading into the wind or not; I was paddling into it at 8:30 a.m. on August 12. With all my weight on my left side, I was sure that the precious little box in my right bathing suit pocket would not be crushed; I just had to keep myself from dropping it into the water (I was cursing myself for not insuring it before leaving Boston). Clover, my beautiful girlfriend of, well, my whole life, was paddling right next me. After battling the winds and tide, we finally pushed our kayaks around a piece of grassy land in the Pamlico Sound and into a quiet little system of inlets. I eyed a little slit of beach and beckoned to Clover to stop. "No," she replied and pointed ahead. Anyone who has kayaked in the sound knows the natural beauty of this area. Unfortunately, I did not care that day.

Most men envision a late night dinner, wine, candles, and romance; their plans include a secluded night at a bed and breakfast or they romantically redo their homes for that special night—all dead giveaways in my book. As we drove down the East Coast to the Virginia Tidewater for my friend's wedding, I knew that I would not have any of those options. We would continue on to Rodanthe, North Carolina after the wedding and spend a romantic week at the beach—with her father, younger brother and sister, and the dogs. We would have our own bedroom of course, the comfort of two cot-like single beds that inhabit the corner of the traditional saltbox on the sea; moreover, I knew Clover would never see this one coming.

My ideas for how to ask the most important person in my life—the woman I had first asked out as a runt-like 8th grader in the playground of the New Paltz Middle School—were limited. I knew I had to find a secluded place to do it...and cheaply. We were grad students, Clover for social work, me for law, and did not have any funds that were not given to us by Aunt Nellie Mae. Then there was my impatience; once I get anything in my head that must me done, it has to be done soon. I stored the ring safely away in the car; my father went through great pains to make the "hiding spot" inconspicuous: a nail box with tissue paper clearly visible through the plastic window. Yet we all knew that Clover was not one to give such things a second look.

On the first morning of our eight-day stay in the most relaxing strip of land in the world, I decided that that would have to be the day—the suspense was killing me! I shook Clover awake at 7:45 and somehow convinced her to go kayaking. Within 40 minutes we had her father's car stacked with two kayaks and were off. Paddling, balancing my body, checking the contents of my pocket, and trying to convince Clover to stop, I steamed ahead of her and jumped onto the beach—actually, a grassless piece of mud (but it would be our mud!). Seeing that I was not going any further, Clover reluctantly came over and joined me.

We were sweaty and hot, but enjoying the beautiful Outer Banks morning; we talked about this and that—I was not listening, but plotting. Finally, I began my proposal (I apologize, but the words are ours and only ours). And with me on my knee (in the mud), she said yes. She cried. We hugged. Besides our wedding day that followed less than a year later, it was our perfect moment.

Then we went back to the cottage and did what all newly engaged people do: we ate breakfast with her father, brother, and sister; played with the dogs; and then had a romantic dinner at the Tiki—with her father, brother, and sister.

And it was perfect.

Why I Had to Show Her the Receipt for the Ring

—Jon Kotcher, business owner, Riverdale, N.Y.

So there I was with a 2 carat ring in the pocket of my bathing suit that once held in a pretty firm stomach but was now being tested for the tensile strength of its threads. After 26 years of marriage, two children, and three years of single life, I was ready to take the plunge again.

I thought I had found my soul mate for the second half of my life. We had been together for about two years and had talked about an engagement and wedding on the beach. After about a half hour of lying in the sun, I was now lobster red. Every two or three minutes I kept grabbing the outside of my pocket to make sure "it" was still there. Finally, convinced that no one would come near the blanket and hoping that there wouldn't be any kids around, I decided my best tactic was to ask Susan to go for a walk.

We walked to an isolated part of the beach where the sand turned to small rocks. Smooth rounded stones from years of waves wearing at their surfaces were still hard on your feet. At 53 years old, somehow the water felt colder and the sand hotter than I remembered when I used to take my kids to the beach. A large retaining cement wall was in back of us and small waves gently moved in and out.

I have always been a romantic and one for surprises. I immediately came up with an idea....I would make believe I had found the ring! "What the hell is that in the water?" I yelled, scooping up some stones and, while palming the ring, exclaiming, "Holy cow! Look at this...I found a ring! This must be a sign from above. Will you marry me?"

What I expected was the old, "Of course I will marry you. I love you!" Instead I got, "That's someone else's ring, Jon. She must be desperate looking for it. We should go right away and turn it into the lost and found."

Ever the quick thinker, I said, "Well, even if it is someone else's, will you marry me?"

"You're kidding?" she said.

I said "No, I'm not kidding," and we hugged and kissed. But I had a really hard time convince Susan that I really had planned this whole event. And she wasn't totally on board until that evening when I showed her the receipt for the ring.

After the Hurricane

—Mike Halminski, wildlife photographer, Waves, N.C.

As for my getting married, we had a date set for Ocracoke Island, October 10. Everything was in place. It was mainly a family-members-only thing, and most everyone had reservations for accommodations near Silver Lake.

Hurricane Isabel changed all that, and the island was closed to visitors for an undetermined amount of time. So we postponed the event, and all reservations canceled. I was getting messages from my side of the family to just go off and do it on our own. Of course, Denise being an outgoing woman, yearns for the event and celebration with family and close friends.

We haven't yet decided what to do. She is getting a little stressed out about it now, which is strange because before the hurricane, I was the one who was stressed about getting married. I couldn't sleep just thinking about it. I was a mess! I told her just to do whatever she wants to do now, although in the back of my mind, it's *Let's just do it privately* (on Ocracoke Island, of course), *get it over with, and have the big celebration later at a convenient time*. I even toyed with the idea of hiring a local fisherman to whisk us away to the island to do it during Ocracoke's solitude of being evacuated. Now the island has just reopened, and we have to replan.

I could devote a big section of a book on the differences in the way men and women envision themselves getting married. The women, it seems, want the fairy tale thing in general, while the guys, for the most part, don't need all the fanfare, and want to get it over with.

We have most everything now to get hitched, including rings and marriage license (good for 60 days). So the pressure is on again. I'll let you know what happens. (See Chapter 14.)

The Last Touch Football Game

—Stu Klein, president, Quantum Group, Montville, N.J.

As the day approached (December 29), I was trying to plan something more fun than the typical rehearsal day festivities. Realizing that the wedding was the end of one era and the start of another, I thought about the defining activities of life as a single guy. For my buddies and me, it was tackle football, ideally played in either snow or mud. So, in planning for the game, I needed some major weather cooperation. With the wedding on a Saturday night, I decided I needed a pretty good snowstorm on the Thursday before. Enough time to clear the roads, but close enough to the date to have "perfect" field conditions. Amazingly, we got exactly that.

So, the morning of the wedding, my groomsmen and assorted male wedding guests got together for what turned out to be the last tackle football game most of us played. With the soft cushion of 6 inches of snow, we had a blast of a game, and then went directly to the rehearsal at noon. Soaked to the skin and a little beat up, we had the rehearsal, showered up, and got ready for the real event.

I guess you could file it under "No matter how old you get, there's nothing like a pick-up game of tackle football to get you ready for married life."

The Wedding Suit

—Myron Adams, writer/ESL teacher, Hughsonville, N.Y.

Polly's mother was quick with her response to our wedding plans, "If what you want is a blood test and a cocktail party, that might work for you, but it doesn't for me." After telling her I might wear an old tweed coat, but get some new leather patches sewn onto its worn elbows, she pronounced, "Oh no you won't!"

When I'd moved to New York a few years before, my father had offered to buy me a Brooks Brothers suit, claiming that every 18-year-old needed one to get a start in life. As a jeans and

T-shirt wearing resident of the East Village, I had little use for three-piece suits. Now, I reconsidered and got the okay to take Dad up on his offer. I approached Brooks Brothers warily, but survived both the stuffy salesman and his chalk-toting tailor who did the fitting. Then, not trusting delivery, I decided to pick up the wedding suit myself at the end of the week.

On the way home that Friday, I didn't want to broadcast my purchase to fellow subway riders, so I tucked the blue and gold box behind my legs. Polly greeted me at the door to our apartment asking, "Where's the suit?" I had left it on the train.

A week later, it felt like old-times being measured for suit number 2. That one, *I* paid for.

Part II
The Long Season: The Engagement Year(s)

Chapter 5

The Give and Go

Okay, let's review:

You did everything you could humanly do to convince her to marry you. You:

1. Took yourself to the next level of commitment and intimacy (which is never to be underestimated).
2. Went out and got the right ring, the one that sparkles like her eyes.
3. Cleaned up better than you might have ever cleaned up before in your life.
4. May have even mustered the courage to speak to her old man.
5. Definitely reached down deeper than you knew you had depth and found the boldness and courage to ask her to marry you!

And in the moment she heard those earth-shaking words, she considered all the prospects out there in the universe…and she looked at the ring…and she looked in your eyes…and she looked inside her heart…and she considered a million and one things that you might never have considered in your life…and then she decided with tears in her eyes and a broad smile on her lovely face that you (yes, you!) are *the* man for her.

You made the team. Congratulations! There's a lot to be pleased about in all that. You've got a right to be proud. A lot of newly engaged men think that the job is essentially done at this point. They've climbed the mountain. They grabbed the brass ring. They brought home the bacon. They even made their dads proud—and their moms gush (unless they're Jewish and in that case their moms grow increasingly ferklempt worrying that their sons might have forgotten something). And now they're exhausted—emotionally and physically.

Now what?

It's quite understandable that a man might conclude that he's earned the right to fall back to the couch, open a beer, put his feet up on the coffee table, and turn on the tube. By all appearances, it looks like all the groom really needs to do is get a haircut, take a shower, put on the monkey suit, and show up at the ceremony on time...and sober...and just dribble down the court for an unchallenged slam dunk. Basically, it feels like the time is right to raise a mug and toast your good self. Not so.

In fact, in my experience (and in interviews with hundreds of brides and grooms), the real work is just beginning. That pre-engagement period is probably similar to running out on the court to the glorious cheers of the crowd than the blood, sweat, and tears you're going to experience firsthand in the ever engaging weeks and months (and, for some, years) of engagement season ahead.

In pushing the basketball metaphor just a little further—and risking moving completely into the absurd realm of fantasy marriage-basketball—just making the cut doesn't guarantee that you're going to be in the starting lineup on the first day of the season. How's that for a sobering thought? Making the cut merely signals the advent of months or years of pre-season practice until you're ready for the real game, which of course is marriage. (I specifically mentioned the word marriage because you'd be surprised at how many men suffer a dramatic disconnect between getting engaged and getting married, as if the one does not necessarily lead into the other.)

Point of order: Michael Halminski, a friend and wildlife photographer from Hatteras Island, North Carolina, who somehow managed to wait until he was 50 years old to get engaged, told me in all sincerity: "I might have thought that I was buying some time before we actually tied the knot, but this thing has taken off without me. It has a life of its own—and it's gaining steam as we go along." (Check out Michael's engagement and wedding stories in Chapters 4 and 14.)

In this period, you're going to find out startlingly new things about yourself and your fiance and your relationship that you never would have suspected before. With the courtship officially over, both of you are more likely to unveil your true colors. And, as such, this is the time that you really do the work in building a solid foundation for the life that you're going to lead with the woman of your dreams.

Don't Get Smug. Don't Be Cocky. No Fancy Moves.

At this point it might be helpful to go back a few chapters and restate the single most elemental truth about the wedding season: Although men and women might share equal urges (emotional, spiritual, sexual, financial, etc.) that drive them to want to spend the rest of their lives together, the actual wedding event is almost always to be found in the domain of the bride-to-be and her mother. (You also might want to reread the Introduction.)

In the vast majority of engagements, men don't have a great deal of emotional investment in the Xs and Os of wedding planning. Keep in mind this is not about what *should* go on in wedding planning, only what *does*. As such, it turns out men are not terribly concerned with what the invitation looks like—or how it reads—or when the save the date card should be mailed—or when the RSVP should be requested.

Men are also typically much less involved than their brides regarding the logistics of the ceremony itself. (An all too typical side of the dialogue: "Just let me know where to stand and what to say and I'll be fine...."). And, by and large, men could care less about location of the reception (the menu, the floral arrangements, the centerpieces, the color scheme, the band, the schedule of events, yadda, yadda, and yadda) than the bride—and her mother. Here again, the simple fact is that, whether by nature or nurture, most women do care about those necessary items in preparing for the wedding.

With all that in mind, we can gain real insight into why there are showers for women, but nothing resembling a shower exists for men—and, in fact, there's no compelling reason to try to explain the omission. And absolutely everybody understands that. Everybody.

Is any of that a problem? No.

But right here is a turning point at which a whole slew of potential relationship problems may, and do, arise. The momentum is shifting and, as such, this is also the point where you have to proceed a little more sensitively and humbly than you might be accustomed to. You have to play a little more controlled.

(*Note:* This might be a little confusing because, true or not, it seemed that one of the things that she really liked about you when you were dating was your boyish swashbuckling irresponsible uncontrolled arrogance. Nevertheless, whether it was previously true or not, I can report that after so many conversations with the women in my classes and the women in my family, it is no longer a turn-on for her. She wants—and needs—you to take off the Zorro costume [or the Jordan jersey] and be the man who will support her through a critical transition in her life.)

Okay, so here's the whole deal laid out in two simple but not-so-easy-to-follow steps:

Step 1: The Fast Break

The first thing today's men must do is to make a startling break from the old team: that is, their fathers, older brothers, and even friends who walked down the long aisle before them. This is obviously more symbolic than actual, but it is a crucial aspect of making for a championship season.

It is unfortunate, in retrospect, but quite clear that previous generations of grooms-to-be made it a practice to dismiss, criticize, patronize and, in effect, ridicule all the work and all the high-end emotions that go into planning a wedding.

Whether the dismissive attitude came of cold feet, embarrassment at appearing soft to one's friends, or the age-old anger at being given orders, men have traditionally shown a genuine disrespect for the wedding preparations. You've seen that blank stare on the faces of your friends and brothers while their fiances or wives speak (it is the male version of the eye roll)...kissing them while they're speaking about things they don't care about (and effectively shutting them up—or not)...smirking along with their smirkful friends while she goes on passionately about choosing the right corsages...scoffing at her anxiety over all the "small stuff"...all of which leads to the worst-case scenario where you blow up with explosive annoyance at her "...obsession with something that's just a party!"

Of course it is not just a party. It is, for her and others, an event of a lifetime...the Super Bowl, the Final Four, and Game Seven all rolled into one. And yes, it is also definitely a party and you should work your butt off trying to figure out how both of you can have a great time at that party.

As you might imagine, all that ridicule—in all its forms—is not received well by the brides-to-be, who, regardless of our intentions, care deeply about each and every aspect of the wedding. And as you might also imagine, the resulting ill-will does not build a firm base upon which to construct a healthy, lasting marriage.

The Beauty of the Give and Go

The solution is not for engaged men to suddenly change who they are. As will be discussed later in the book, no one should ever deny or cover up who he or she is in a relationship—and we all know the futility of trying to escape oneself and be someone else. However, in a dramatic break from the past, it is long past time for men to stop the battle of the sexes and begin to learn how to validate the women who will share their lives—and, of course, learn to appreciate the vast amount of energy that goes into making a wedding a successful event.

Just as we would hope that our typically male interests in sports, cars, mountain climbing, or beer making (name your vice) would not be put down as childish by the women we love (which, unfortunately, they often do), we would serve our women and our marriages well if we accepted their passions as well. Just as they don't have to learn to play golf or to love football as much as our good friends—though it's fine if they do—we don't have to love wedding preparations. We don't even have to like them. We just have to take part in a respectful and present way. Indeed, the wedding season is, for many of us, the first opportunity to learn how to support the women we love for who they are—even if we don't understand their fervor.

Step 2: Role Playing

Here the basketball metaphor works particularly well. In this early phase of the engagement season, it's best to understand your role on the wedding team. You are not the big man inside, nor are you the go to guy at the end of the game. You're not even the point guard setting up the final play. You are a role player—arcing the ball to the big man inside so she can slam it down, grabbing a rebound and swinging it out to the go to guy behind the line, helping the point guard set up the play in the backcourt. You are the shooting guard, the small forward, the sixth man off the bench, the man who sets up the pick—absolutely necessary to the effective functioning of the team effort. But please understand that you are not going to be giving ESPN—or the Wedding Channel—interviews in the locker room at the end of the game.

Although many men subscribe to the "You're either on the bus or off the bus" philosophy of life (Translation: I'm either running the show or I'm watching television), this phase of the season puts us in a true supporting role. It's a good one to learn because a good marriage is—for better not worse—a partnership in every sense of the word. Sometimes she takes the lead and he supports her. Sometimes he takes the lead and she supports him. More often than not, though, husband and wife cross the finish line hand in hand. As it should be.

I suspect that the most miserable husbands in the world are the ones who think they're the George Steinbrenners of holy matrimony. They consider themselves the kings of their castles, the general managers of their teams, CEOs of the household, or whatever other silly manifestations of your run-of-the-mill control freak. Literature is replete with the tragedies of men who take themselves too seriously: my starting lineup for the Hubris All-Stars is Cain, Othello, Helmer Torvald, King Lear, Stanley Kowalski, and Eddie Carbone.

Off the stage and on the street, however, they are the ones sitting around the bar at the local tavern a few years into the marriage growling into their beers about the "ball and chains." They are also the ones most likely to confide in their mistresses (when the marriage is falling apart) lame excuse that "she doesn't understand me." They remind me of an upwardly mobile corporate guy I met a while back at the local health club (he had a beautiful wife, two sweet looking kids, made-for-TV dog, big job, a deep blue BMW roadster) who sincerely confided to me after a game of racquetball that "This is the only time in my life that I am happy." How pathetic is *that*?

And I knew before we were two more sentences into our conversation that he hated his home because of all the pressure he put upon himself to be the king—to be right ALL the time. It's a very dangerous temptation to make yourself—or your self-image—more important than you really are—or need to be. Resist it.

Look in Her Mirror

And the way to resist it is to take a long hard look in the mirror and see yourself how your fiance sees you. Not how you see yourself. She loves you for who you are—and how you give her the support and affirmation to be who she is.

And in this Cinderella of a season, you have the opportunity to support her dreams—and in doing so, make your own dreams come true. It takes practice and almost other worldly control, but it is definitely worth it. Just like your old soccer coach or piano teacher would chant: Practice, practice, practice every day.

For many of us, being supportive does not come naturally. Try envisioning yourself as the foundation of the house, the driver of the black limousine, the 300-pound lineman, the guy on the bench who waves the towel and whips up the crowd.

There will be times over the long engagement season (no matter how long it actually is and no matter how smoothly it seems to be going) when the world seems to be spinning off its axis. This is when she needs you to be the man she believes she is marrying: a partner, someone who puts her happiness first.

Chapter 6

The Game Plan:

Know Your Job. Know Your Place. Smile A Lot.

Somewhere along the way, you must've heard the Serenity Prayer or one of its endless variations: *God grant me the serenity to accept the things I cannot change, the courage to change the things I can, and the wisdom to know the difference.*

Although the passage is as overused as the old pre- and post-game "We're just taking it one day at a time," it is not bad advice under any circumstances—and I'd have to say that it's especially useful during the long pre-wedding season. Useful enough, that is, that you should commit it to memory along with other essential facts of life such as Michael Jordan's original uniform number, your mother's birthday, and the anniversary of when you and your sweetie started going out. It's that important. To move through all the engagement traffic with a serene Buddha-like smile means that you're going to need all the patience you can muster.

As I mentioned in the previous chapter, the key concept to understand when planning for the wedding is that the groom is not expected (or wanted) to be the foreman or the CEO. However, he must do what is expected of him—and do it well.

Just a gentle reminder stolen from the Introduction before we go any further: Although you are an integral and irreplaceable part of the event itself, this wedding is not *entirely* about you. Nor is it *a lot* about you. A great deal of planning has already gone into your wedding day that—I guarantee—predates your arrival on the scene (perhaps even by a few decades). As such, while it's terribly important for you to have a real grasp of everything that goes into making this a most memorable occasion, it is equally important to know that you are a role player on the betrothal team—the sixth man off the bench—and, of course, that you know what that role might be. Finally, please keep in mind these two things:

1. In those categories from which you are traditionally excluded, you may not only be invited (or expected) to participate, but may need to make you preferences known. That's absolutely fine. This is the new millennium and the decisions belong to the both of you.
2. In those categories from which your fiance is traditionally excluded, you may want her input, or she may wish to have a voice in the decisions. This is, again, fine.

The following is the short list of duties that must be performed in order to make The Day as successful as your bride—and her mother—have always dreamt it to be.

(Key: *The letters following each item reflect who should be in on the decision: Bride (B), Mother of the Bride (MB), Groom (G), Mother of the Groom (MG). Please also note the conspicuous absence of your dad and her dad from the list. Aside from the initial, largely ceremonial, asking for her father's blessings (see Chapter 1)—and much much later, his unceremonial signing of the checks—most dads ride the pine for all the essential planning phases of this wedding. Dads may travel with the management team and may even serve in various capacities according to the terms of their own marriage contracts, but mostly they just get their orders from the Joint General Managers (your mother and your future mother-in-law) and try to stay out of the way of the real movers and shakers.*)

1. Set a date. (B, MB, G, MG)
2. Reserve a site for the ceremony (church, reception hall, inn, beach, dolphin tank, or whatever). (B, MB, and occasionally G)
3. Make a guest list. (B, MB, G, MG)
4. Book a reception location (if different from the ceremony site). (B, MB, and rarely, G)
5. Get a caterer. (Generally MB)

6. Arrange for music—deejay or band. (B, G)
7. Order invitations. (B, MB, G) You probably don't care unless you're in the printing business, but you have to go along with the CEO and CFO—and offer some opinions.)
8. Order flowers (B, MB, G)As with the invitations business, but you don't have to go along. In fact, they probably don't want you there, because you simply don't understand why table arrangements are so important—and they don't have the language to explain it to you.)
9. Book a photographer. (B, MB)
10. Register for gifts. (B, MB)
11. Buy a Wedding Dress. (B, MB)
12. Arrange for tuxedo rentals. (G)
13. Book a honeymoon. (B, G)
14. Get a limosine—or arrange for your Uncle Murray's Chrysler. (G)
15. Attendants. (B)
16. Ushers. (G—but get help)
17. Gifts for attendants and ushers. (B, G—with advice)
18. Prepare a speech/vows. (G)

As I'm sure you've already noted, with some unspoken measure of relief, there are only eight definite jobs for the groom here (with an additional possible two or three others where you're supposed to help). So, let's look more closely at the groom's Xs and Os for the big game:

Set a Date (B, MB, G, MG)

Everybody has got to be on the same page for this one. As all good contractors, stockbrokers, air-traffic controllers, wedding planners, and point guards know, timing is everything. This is particularly true for a wedding, which one hopes one will only have to do once in lifetime. As such, the four cocaptains must check and double check to see that the date and time are in complete synch, both in terms of essential guests and facility availability. (Plus, if it's important to someone important, the astrological signs for that day should be consulted—and respected.)

While it doesn't really matter that cousin Honora or Uncle Arnold won't be able to make it to the wedding, if one of the organizers doesn't do his or her job and it turns out that the best man will be on his own honeymoon or Gramma Tootie is scheduled for hip replacement, the proverbial cow pie is going to hit the fan. And, as I'm sure it is writ in spiritual texts worldwide, the resulting stink will permeate the walls of your marriage house for decades.

The organizing team must make sure that every member of the wedding party will be willing and able to attend the ceremony. That includes all members of the A+ version of the A list (see next page): siblings, grandparents, favorite cousins, bridesmaids, groomsmen, etc. And, lest you forget that they all need some place to go to drop off the presents, you'd be well-advised to be absolutely certain that the church/reception hall is available when they are.

For your part, you need only be certain that you know whom you are responsible for on the list. In most instances, your sole responsibility will be your own family, the best man, and ushers. Whomever you must consult, however, the critical piece is to know in advance who is essential to the success of your day—and who can just as well wish you well from their "previous engagement."

(*Hint:* When discussing wedding dates with your best man and ushers, make sure they have their date books open or are in front of the Palm Pilot—and make sure they actually write it down. Ten months later, you don't want them choosing between your wedding and a Lakers' game or a date with "…the most beautiful girl I have ever laid my eyes on.")

(*Another Hint:* Call your best man and ushers in monthly intervals anyway to remind them that it's still on.)

Make a Guest List (B, MB, G, MG)

As you might imagine, this is as much an economic decision as it is a personnel one. Each individual who comes to your wedding not only adds to the cost of the event, but plays a singularly minor if significant role in determining where the ceremony and party will take place—another brick in the wedding wall. A lot of people will be trying out for the team, so there has got to be some cuts.

The bottom line on the guest list, which you might want to think of as kind of like NBA draft day, is that it can only be compiled after you've determined:

1. Who's paying for the wedding.
2. How much that person is willing to shell out.
3. What his or her conditions for the wedding might be.
4. How you and your bride envision the biggest day of your lives.

Don't let anyone tell you what you and your bride want. It is your day. That said, keep in mind that if you have decided on a big, BIG wedding in a simple setting or a small but elegant affair in a pricey castle on the banks of a gently flowing river in the south of France, the guest list game plans are radically different. Although you might want every friend you've ever had to come celebrate your good fortune, keep in mind that every guest adds to the final bill.

Of course, whoever is paying for the wedding generally has the biggest voice in how many people will be invited, but that is not always the case. Get that part straight right away—and don't be vague about it. In any event, you and your family will be given a general number of guests that will be okay to invite—and that's generally half to three-quarters of the total number.

However you and your fiance (and, in some cases, your fiance's mother) conceive of this wedding, so, one good place to start is to make guests lists according to the following formula:

A+ List

Absolutely, positively, unequivocally, must be there. Unless you're going to elope, you have no choice when it comes to this group. The A+ list always includes immediate family, grandparents, and closest friend(s). It's important to write down this list because it is your baseline; the wedding will never ever get any smaller than this unless you elope.

Also, when figuring headcounts for the invitations list and reception, don't forget to include all the members of the wedding party, including the often-overlooked ringbearer's and flower girl's parents—and yourselves! Don't laugh. It happens.

A List

These are the ones you really want—or need to have—at your wedding. This group includes most of the rest of your aunts, uncles, and first cousins (or at least those you've seen in the past 10 years), good friends from high school and college, and friends/associates whose good cheer you feel you need to make the day absolutely right. Or, barring that, those you owe big-time for things you may or may not want to share with your fiance. This group may also include your boss and/or various close relatives whom you might actually despise but must be there to preserve the peace in the family—or your income. (You already know who I'm talking about, so just suck it up and put the name down on the roster.)

B List

These are the casual friends, neighbors, daily business associates, and extended family members whom you'd consider inviting to a big open house, but don't necessarily want to host for an intimate dinner or share a summer cottage on Block Island. These B-listers include teammates from the high school championship soccer team, fraternity brothers, drinkin' buddies from the Old Dutch Tavern, former girlfriends (be *very* careful here), second cousins and beyond, your bookie, neighbors, close business associates, your shrink, and, of course, all those folks who have, for one inexplicable reason or another, invited you to their weddings.

(*Another Hint:* Whoever doesn't get invited to your wedding will not be inviting you to theirs.)

C List

The C-listers are the people whose phone numbers you don't know—and whose last (or first) names are not always on the tip of your tongue. They include all those business associates on your Christmas Rolodex and coworkers who don't know where you live and wouldn't be able to pick your bride out of a book of wedding mug shots. It also includes the doorman, the guy in the parking lot, the accountant at the firm in Passaic, and the nice balding guy on the commuter train who once offered you a ride home when your car broke down. This list should be invoked only if you are intent on having the biggest affair anyone's ever seen in Highland Park, Illinois—and, of course, someone's got the capital to foot the enormous bill. Or if you're not quite as popular as you think you are and practically everyone on the A and B lists turn you down—and you still want to have a big affair.

Arrange for Music—Deejay or Band (B, G)

Your mother wants a salsa group. Your father-in-law wants the one-man band he saw at the Elks fundraiser last March. Your cousin Carmine knows the bass player on an up-and-coming metal group out of Astoria. Your fiance's sensitive sister has put in her vote for Sinead O'Connor. Grandma wants the new Gene Krupa orchestra led by that charming horn player Dale DeMarco. Grandpa, who has recently undergone a personality change, wants that hip-hop deejay named Crappy Crap.

Don't listen to any of them. This is a more important decision than first meets the eye. Not only do you have to dance with a smile to their particular brand of music for three hours, but the deejay or band leader is more than likely going to serve as the emcee or host for the evening's events. She or he will, in effect, choose the tone for the evening, regardless of how laid back, elegant, campy, or trashy the reception environment might seem. So, choose wisely (and *do not* allow your cousin Kenny, who just got his first deejay gig or whose band just made their debut at the Zodiac Lounge, near the microphone).

First, as always, determine your budget. Everything follows from that. And don't break the bank on a band, unless it's someone like Tom Petty or U2—and even then you might not want a group that takes the limelight away from the happy couple. Honestly, the music is one of the last things anyone remembers from a wedding—unless it is atrocious. All you need is music people can dance to.

Second, assemble a list of bands and deejays that work for that number—or near that number. As my Uncle Max would say, everything is negotiable.

Third, take the time to go see every venue that seems to fit your vision of the kind of music and the demeanor of evening you want. Everyone who makes a living working on a stage has a smooth patter in the interview—and a videotape that makes them look like they've been headlining in Vegas—so it's critical to actually go and watch them in wedding action. See who matches your view of the kind of wedding you want.

As I'm sure you already know, there is a remarkably wide range of wedding performers. You'll have a pick of everything from the smooth be-tuxed Lawrence-Welkish bandleader playing dentist office music while making deeply resonant patriotic or religious pronouncements all the way to the high school dropout, turned meth freak, turned radio deejay, turned religious convert loaded with caffeine and a natural Christian high who comes equipped with party hats, leis, noisemakers, fake noses, and then fills the evening with games, one-liners, practical jokes, and a final gooey rendition of your favorite Karen Carpenter medley. Get a deejay or band who works for you, not the other way around.

Fourth, if you're opting for a band, find someone who can play your song exactly how you want it played. Further, if you want a deejay, get his or her complete playlist.

Fifth, regardless of whom you choose, you and your fiance can—and should—choose your own playlist.

My son Cael had a deejay that played the theme from *Rocky* as our family entered the large hotel reception hall. Judging from that, you might imagine he was a genuine presence on the stage, a showman—exactly what Melissa's mom and dad wanted from the evening. He was indeed very memorable, and it was a lot of fun. In contrast, my daughter Nancy, who had a 175 guest wedding on the lawn of a beautiful 18th century inn near our upstate home, hired a somewhat self-effacing hipster deejay from Woodstock who played all the songs she and Michael wanted, made all the announcements in a reserved manner and disappeared when the evening was over. I have no memory of what he looked like—or what he sounded like. For them, he was perfect. Another vision altogether comes from my daughter Addie, who got married on the beach on Hatteras Island in the presence of family and very few friends. She used a boom box and allowed select members of the family to choose CDs as we ate tons of shrimp and danced for hours on the broad deck of the Moon Over Hatteras Restaurant in Rodanthe. Again, it was exactly what she wanted. It was perfect. Finally, Clover, who got married by the stream in our backyard, had her reception at the local micro-brewery, the Gilded Otter, with music provided by the house band—Kars and Bars. They did covers of every song Clover and Jeffrey ever made out to while growing up. They were perfect. Even better than perfect—the dance floor was never empty.

Arrange for Tuxedo Rentals (G)

Yup. No Bs, no MBs, no MGs. It's all groom. The tuxes go on your back—and your boys' backs—so this job is all yours. It's actually your best man's job, but since he's your job, you have to make sure it gets done.

Before we go any further, please understand that there is absolutely no requirement that anybody wear a tux at your wedding. Also, in requiring formal wear, please understand that you are requiring your groomsmen to cough up somewhere in the neighborhood of $100 or more to rent a tux. Make sure they can afford it—or you can afford it if they can't.

However, if you decide that you and your ushers will go tuxless, it is also imperative that you establish a clear, unambiguous wedding dress policy: Dark suit, white shirt, and tie will serve you very well. Without a dress policy, your old buddy Doots might show up in his favorite "dress up" Metallica T-shirt. Or old Scott from Tau Kappa Epsilon, who is regarding your wedding as a golden opportunity to score, may arrive in his *Sopranos* chick-magnet ensemble. And someone will show up in a Mickey Mouse or naked lady tie. Picture it. Prevent it.

That said, there are two phases to this tuxedo rental job: (1) choosing the style of tux, and (2) making sure that everyone who needs one, gets one (and one that fits).

When choosing a style, your local tuxedo rental store will have a wide range of looks—and prices. Keeping in mind your budget (and your ushers' ability to pay) and the sizes of all those being measured, I would suggest first asking your fiance to help you choose appropriate attire. She's your partner; find out how she envisions the wedding party.

If that's not in the game plan (and you're a brave soul), then I recommend looking yourself in the mirror and really determining what your style is. A little self-knowledge never hurt anybody. You don't want to show up in top hat and tails if you're really a mullet, untied Timberlands kind of guy. If you have blond hair, a sailor's ruddy tan, and a diploma on your wall from Princeton, you don't want a zoot suit. You just end up looking doofy. Keep this rule first and foremost in your mind: You don't want to look goofy. The paisley or light blue number with frilly shirt may look good (or campy or outrageous) today, but in 20 years, when your kids gather around to view the parents' wedding album, you are going to look like a big flaming jackass. I promise.

Unless you're getting married in your Ocean Pacific board shorts on a balmy beach, choose something classic and understated. In fact, don't aim to make a statement of any kind. You'll never regret it. I, who wore a white linen suit to my own wedding in New Orleans, insisted on having the hem of the pants barely touching the tops of my shoes (as in the style of the day, I must let you know) so that my socks flashed with every step I took—and, if that wasn't bad enough, I also insisted on complementing my shortened pants with my brown dress hipster boots. As you can clearly see in the accompanying photograph, my wedding will forever be a public embarrassment to my children. I can forgive myself by saying I was only 22 years old—and barely that—but, that said, I do regret the look mightily.

Be sure that everyone in the wedding party has a tux that pretty much fits him. That means that everyone must go in for a fitting. In other words, don't rely on your friends to know their measurements—they don't—and, as seems to be the case worldwide, your father and your father-in-law most likely think that they still fit into that 42 regular that they wore to someone's bar mitzvah back in 1969. They don't. You just don't want the best men in your life looking like they just walked off the set of the *Three Stooges*.

A reasonably good idea is to invite everyone to a "fitting party" followed by a game of pool or b-ball or a trip to the neighborhood tavern. But don't call it a party. And don't call it date. Call it "I'll meet you at ____'s—and then we'll go to ____'s to order the tuxes."

If the wedding is to be held in another state or country, or if you have groomsmen coming in from out of town, please know that there is a simple way to avoid traveling with a tux or paying extended rental fees. Almost all tux rental shops have a sort of unspoken reciprocal agreement with other shops around the globe. If they want you to return for a local wedding (which they will), they'll measure you for free—and then all you need to do is to send the numbers to the tux shop in the wedding city.

Book a Honeymoon (B, G)

The universe is loaded with wonderful honeymoon spots—from the Motel 6 in a neighboring town, to a grass hut on a deserted beach in Tahiti, to a $3,000 a night suite in Paris. There are only two rules about choosing wedding locales:

1. Be sure you *both* really want to go there. It must be romantic first and joyful second. Anything else is gravy. You don't want to be dealing with decades of disappointment (trust me on this one) if one of you isn't happy with the choice.

2. Be sure you have the cash (or a benefactor) to do exactly what you want. You don't want to nickel and dime your way through your first few days of marriage—and you also don't want to incur a debt that you'll still be paying off while your kids are applying to college. If you can't find the "perfect place" to match your budget, choose one of the million and one wonderful vacation spots on the globe—and then look dreamily in her eyes and promise her that you'll go to paradise for your 20th Anniversary. It's got a nice, eternal ring to it.

(Read Chapter 10 for more about honeymoons.)

Get a Limo (G)

...or arrange for your Uncle Murray's Cadillac with the Norstar system.

Although the cute little Renault and the clunky bush Land Cruiser in *Four Weddings and a Funeral* were very charming, they're not charming at a real wedding—especially if you're in evening clothes and your new wife is wearing something that costs more than $1,000 and requires its own closet. You're best off driving—or being driven in—something that can easily and cleanly accommodate tuxedos, fancy dresses, and, of course, massive wedding gowns.

Along the same lines, I am sorry, but your old lovable, beat-to-crap VW Rabbit won't do, nor will your buddy's Corvette, nor will Cousin Myron's Dodge Tradesman "Love Machine." Get a sedan, a Cadillac, a Chrysler, a Lincoln, a Benz, a Lexus, or an Audi. Get as late a model as possible. This is not about your image. It's about dirt and grease and rust and her dress and your jacket.

The only rule from there is to make sure you know exactly where you're going every step of the way. The Cadillac Norstar system—or any of its variants—is excellent. If that option is not in the cards—or the wallet—get explicit directions from each place to each place on the Internet. Don't fall into the typical sitcom male trap of assuring your exasperated mate, "I know where I'm going," when you simply don't know where the hell you are. Sometimes we just don't know—and your wedding is a bad place to find that out.

Next, if you can't—or don't want to—find a good, big, clean sedan, arrange for a limo or a town car. Prices vary ridiculously, so shop around and question folks who have used the service before. Make sure the outfit has more than one car. Make sure you get a written guarantee about time and mileage vs. price. The benefits to having a car and driver are manifold—there are fewer things to think about and you can safely assume you won't get lost. At the very end of the night there will be someone who is not drunk to drive you off to your night of bliss.

One more thing: On a strictly personal level, I would strongly suggest avoiding the understandable temptation to rent a stretch Hummer. The "regular" sized Humvees are not only the most ridiculous vehicles on paved roads, but the stretch ones will make you look like you're going to the junior prom (which means that they've probably been puked in so many times that the smell of antibacterial shampoos will be enough to make *you* want to puke).

Best Man and Ushers (G and G Alone)

Choosing the best man is sometimes tricky, especially if you have a whole battalion of good buddies, but rest assured the process is not nearly as tricky as choosing a maid of honor. So relax, you don't have to get real touchy-feely here. There are rules, albeit largely unwritten until now.

Here's the Deal in Choosing a Best Man:

1. If you live below the Mason-Dixon Line (in particular, North Carolina), your best man is often your dad. (I don't get it, but it makes the decision much easier.)

2. If you live anywhere else in the country and have a brother and he's not in jail, he's your best man.

3. If you have two or more brothers, but only one is out of high school, the oldest one is your best man.

4. If you have two or more brothers and two or more are out of high school—and none of them are in jail—you can choose your best friend. In fact, in the interests of family harmony, your old elementary, middle school, high school, or college buddy will do very well. Please note that you don't have to be blood brothers with this guy—it's not necessary or recommended that you ever cut yourselves and press the wounds together—as long as he is reliable and cleans up okay, he's your man.

5. As in number 4, you can choose your best friend, but not if he chokes in front of crowds, or is a bad drunk, or has a bad speech impediment. I know that last piece may not be PC in today's world, but please keep in mind that the best man must give at least one speech—and probably two—and you could find yourself in the middle of a flushing toilet if any of those conditions are present. (Note: Unfortunately, if your only brother is afflicted with one of those mis-attributes, you must still choose him for the sake of family unity.)

Choosing Ushers

Regarding the choice of ushers, my team of wedding advisors reports that there are typically six ushers supporting the groom at a traditional wedding, but that number has no basis in cultural precedent or fact. It's not in the Bible or the Koran. Miss Manners doesn't play the numbers. Choose your best boys, the ones you'd like to play basketball or pool with, the ones you'd like to drive Route 66 with, the ones you can count on to help you move furniture no matter how hungover they might be. But I'd recommend keeping the number down to somewhere in the range of a basketball or hockey starting lineup. A big crowd up at the altar looks like you're trying too hard. Or you need too much help getting yourself up there.

There are three simple rules for establishing inclusion into you Usher fraternity:

1. Brothers (yours and hers) first.
2. Friends second.
3. If you have an open space, choose your cousin Kenny, the one you wouldn't let take pictures or videos or be the deejay. It's your random act of kindness for the day and it might even enhance your karma. It will also make Grandma very happy.

Gifts for Ushers and Best Man (G—With Advice)

According to my daughter Addie, who is hotwired to the Martha Stewart social rules index, and supported by several wedding planners, you must buy a gift for each of the groomsmen—and it should be presented to them at the rehearsal dinner.

Generally, this is a one-stop-shopping event; everyone gets the same gift. The usual gifts are engraved mugs, champagne flutes, tie clasps, flasks, money clips, key chains, knives, pens, etc. On the more nontraditional level side, I've also heard of tickets to Red Sox games, special CDs (or DVDs), inscribed books, etc. The important thing is to remember that they are tokens of your gratitude, not to be confused with measures of your gratitude—and as such should not cost an arm and a leg.

And just in case you're thinking of it, no joke presents. Even if it's a very good joke. I'm not going to give you any ideas because it's just possible some of you might like one of them so well that you'll go ahead and do it anyway. Keep in mind that someone special, such as your wife-to-be (or the transcendent part of you waiting to be her husband) will be hurt ever so slightly by the flipness of the gesture. It's definitely not worth the brief chuckle it will produce.

Prepare a Speech and Your Vows (G)

The Wedding Ceremony Speech

Depending on the capacity of your two families to endure a heartfelt speech intended to make everyone laugh or cry while they're already weeping copiously at the beautiful vision of you two getting married right in front of their eyes, you are certainly free to compose some words for those assembled in your honor. You are also certainly free to say nothing; it's not expected and, as I've been informed by several experienced wedding-goers, many of your guests will appreciate your dignified silence.

If you decide to speak to the guests at the ceremony, however, please follow these general guidelines:

1. As with the wedding proposal, keep it short and sweet. The pageant itself and the actual vows are more important and more eternal than any words that might be spoken at this time.

2. It's best to commit your thoughts to memory, but if that is not possible, don't write them on paper ripped from your high school or college spiral notebook. Find a sheet of clean white paper, write the speech neatly and large enough so that you can read it without stumbling while sweat or tears are flowing down your cheeks, and then fold it only enough times so that it will fit into the inside pocket of your jacket.

3. Don't say anything—not even a single seemingly inconsequential word—that might embarrass your fiance or your family at that remarkably solemn moment. You also don't want to embarass yourself in the years to follow when you replay the videotape and your kids hear you say things you'd never allow them to say in your presence.

The Vows

A lot of couples write their own vows. I always find this to be a touching and very meaningful part of the ceremony. As with the speeches, though, it is not necessary nor is it expected. The minister/rabbi/judge has it all under control if you're not inclined to create your own ceremony. Without question, the traditional vows (in which you repeat the age-old promise to love, honor, and cherish your beloved) are some of the most beautiful words ever constructed in the English language—and, as such, are definitely hard to beat for pure momentousness.

If you choose to write your own vows, however, follow these guidelines:

1. Keep them short and, above all, dignified. There are few times in our lives when we get a chance to express our deepest feelings to those who truly want to hear them, so take this opportunity to rise up above the smallness of the world and say something true and eternal.
2. Look in her eyes. Speak the words directly to her, not the guests. They don't count.
3. Speak your own words from your own heart. Don't quote anybody. Don't ask anybody to write the words for you. Unlike the proposal, which you could model because no one else will ever hear it, the vows must be utterly unique to you. I'm not offering scripts because you don't want someone recognizing it from her cousin Stella's wedding. Somehow you will say you love her with all your heart. Somehow you will say that you ll love her till the end of time. That should do it.

Chapter 7

Contract Time:
Who Used to Be a Millionaire?

What you need to know is that this affair—no matter how small and intimate or big and grand—is going to cost someone you know a whole lot of money. The only questions are who and how much.

Your father probably told you thousands of times that money doesn't grow on trees. He may also have stuck out that thick finger and muttered something along the lines of, "The good things in life don't come cheap." (My guess is that he said that right after your mother sweetly warbled something along the lines of, "The best things in life are free.") And if he's anything like my Depression-era dad, you know (by heart) what he made at his first job, the rent on his first apartment, the cost of his first Chevy Impala, the price of gasoline in 1962, and exactly why you're paying too much for everything you buy.

It is quite likely, however, that your old man never told you how much he paid for your sister's wedding—or, in the case of a sisterless life, how much Uncle Morty paid for your homely cousin Sheila's wedding. Real men don't talk present salary—or wedding costs. As financial whiz Ruth Hayden told me, "People are more comfortable talking about their sex lives than about their money." (See Chapter 8.)

More than likely, the old man just did one of three things:

1. Shrugged his shoulders and said, "What could I do? She's my little girl."
2. Looked you in the eye and muttered, "I offered to buy them a house, but no, she wanted a *big* wedding."
3. Turned his back and walked out of the room.

So it's not surprising that almost all men enter the engagement season without a clue as to how much the damages will actually be. Try thinking of it this way: You're standing in a parking lot somewhere glaring at the big ugly scrape you just found on your fender. You have absolutely no idea what it's going to cost, but you have a sinking feeling that it's going to be much more than you would ever guess in your wildest dreams.

And, let us be honest, you are right. Wedding planning involves the word guests...and guests don't come cheap.

So let's go to the videotape: The open house party you and your roommate/girlfriend threw last year to watch the Super Bowl or to celebrate the last *Survivor* show, probably cost $200 in chips, soda, beer, wine, and liquor. Just add a lot more people, dinner for everyone, drinks, music for three to four hours, wedding attire, limos, and...two more zeros and you'll end up with the average cost of an American wedding in the new millennium. That's $20,000, in case you're lost—and keep in mind that's just the average (which includes all those folks who get hitched at City Hall and then go out for Chinese with a couple of friends).

Who Pays; Who Plays

As you are probably aware, the bride's parents are traditionally the ones who foot the entire bill for the wedding. In that gilded age-old scenario, the groom's family gets off "cheap" by taking care of the rehearsal dinner—and nothing else.

However, as you've no doubt observed, the culture is changing at a remarkably rapid pace. As Bob Dylan told us, "The first ones now will later be last; The times they are a-changin." The nuclear family is not what it once was; gender roles in love and work are profoundly different than they once were; and couples are marrying later and later (and later) in life. Even that cheap rehearsal dinner has grown from an informal gathering of the wedding party alone to a far more formal event that can and does include practically everyone who has driven more than 19.9 miles to get to the affair. So, while it's probably true that many brides' parents still want to (or think they should) be the ones who pay for the wedding, it is no longer safe to assume it will be that way.

More and more, according to the Website of Richard Markel, director of the Association for Wedding Professionals (*www.afwpi.com*), the wedding costs are being shared by the couple and one or both—or, in the case of multiple divorces, several—sets of parents. Indeed, increasing numbers of couples are simply paying for and managing their own weddings. They know exactly what they want—and are not willing to compromise with anyone else on how it is to proceed.

Axiom

She or he who pays for a wedding gains control of most, if not all, of the major decisions regarding the circumstances of the affair. Money does talk. Of course, it is in everyone's best interest to be sensitive to the wishes and dreams of those intimately involved in the celebration. But the bottom line is that the persons who control the money will have the final say on practically all arrangements. Keep in mind, too, that many dads think it is their duty to pay for their daughter's weddings. If you don't allow them that, you'll be injuring them in ways you might not understand for decades. Above all, be thoughtful and good-natured.

So, who pays for the affair must be discussed early in the engagement period—and the terms must be spelled out clearly enough to avoid any misunderstandings later on. This part can get very sticky, depending on expectations, financial health, disparity in income between the two families, religious requirements, etc.

My suggestion is that when you two announce your engagement to families and friends, you should initially avoid identifying any date—or even a loose timetable—for the wedding. Just tell everyone, "We're working on it," and then give them that goofy we're-so-in-love smile. Not even the most cold-hearted person can yell at you while you're in the throes of that smile. This will also temporarily keep mothers and mothers-in-law from getting into that high torque wedding gear from which there is no return and it will allow the two of you a brief, if delusional, feeling that you'll be blissfully engaged forever.

Then later (a week, a month, no later than three months), when the giddiness of your engagement begins to wane ever so slightly—or enough that you both understand the value of a dollar again—you and your fiancé need to sit down and discuss what you really want from your wedding. You two alone. Nobody else.

Then you two alone (that is, nobody else), need to figure out what it will cost and whether you're interested in or capable of paying for it. Then go to the parents. And in giving a nod to tradition, speak to her parents first, then to yours. Find out what they are willing—and able—to pay for at the affair. Then decide how much money or debt you are willing—and able—to add to that amount. You will then be ready to make the real decisions about your wedding.

Estimating the Actual Costs of Your Wedding

According to the Association of Bridal Consultants, in the year 2000 the average American wedding (150 guests) ran about $19,000. That's for the traditional package (rehearsal dinner, ceremony, and reception) that generally takes place within a 48-hour period. We're not talking three-day gonzo affairs at Camp Getaway in the Berkshires or at Warwick Castle in the lovely Cotswalds or if you spring for the whole group traveling to Belize, or, even more romantically, the Tuscan coast of Italy. I'm also not talking champagne breakfasts the day before and the morning after the big *I Do*.

Nothing is cheap about a wedding. When our daughters Nancy, Addie, and Clover were making their relatively modest wedding plans, it seemed that Patti and I were writing checks for $1,000 every time we turned around. In fact, in retrospect there was actually no *seem* about it, we actually were writing thousand-dollar checks to everyone remotely involved in the weddings. And please note that we live in upstate New York, not Manhattan or Chicago or Los Angelos.

The Myth of the Cheap Backyard Wedding

Before I go any further, let me first disavow you of the naïve assumption that a backyard wedding/barbeque is going to be a cheap alternative. Sorry.

The backyard barbeque that George Banks (played by Steve Martin) envisioned when first approached in *Father of the Bride* may certainly be less expensive than holding the reception at the local wedding mill, but that's only if you're talking chips, hot dogs, hamburgers, Bud Lite, Shop-Rite brand soda, paper plates, plastic forks and spoons, cousin Kenny commandeering the CD player, overflowing toilets, and a genuine willingness to cut the Grand Union sheet cake in the event of pouring rain and gloppy mud.

If, however, you're thinking more along the lines of a big tent, caterer, real tables and chairs, a band, a three-tier wedding cake, wine that doesn't come in cartons, Porta-Potties that don't smell, and some outward semblance of taste and order, then the traditional lawn or backyard wedding can easily cost as much—or more—than you'll find at most reception facilities.

The original plan for the wedding of our daughter Nancy was to hold it in our near idyllic backyard in the middle of the vast green woods at the base of the Shawangunk Mountains in upstate New York. Nice, right? The vision itself was beautiful to behold: She and Michael would take their vows in the vine covered gazebo I had built years before at the edge of the gurgling stream—and then we'd all eat and drink and dance the night away under the glittering stars.

Not so. At a very friendly meeting with Bruce Kasan, a very nice, very talented, and very reasonable local restaurateur, we learned that the simple idyllic backyard wedding we envisioned (complete with authentic North Carolina barbeque) would cost us the equivalent of a big addition to the house, a brand new BMW 325ci, or a 28-foot Chris-Craft. Everything beyond the singularly impressive food and drink estimate for 175 people, Bruce gently informed us, would have to be rented. That is, the parking attendants, the Porta-Potties, the big tent, and every single thing in it. Every chair, fork, spoon, glass, tablecloth, etc., had a price tag on it.

Patti and I had not yet actually recovered from our collective gasp when Bruce, perhaps not adequately sensing the pending medical emergency, stuck a fork in the proceedings and turned them over. It was done within seconds of his suggestion that the backyard had too much of a slope for dining and dancing—and that we might consider having some fill brought in to level the property. (He was kind and wise enough at the time to omit the estimated cost of sod or reseeding.)

So, Nancy and Michael were married for approximately half the price on the other side of the mountain...on the manicured grounds of the quaint and beautiful Hasbrouck House Inn in charming

Stone Ridge, New York. (By the way, Clover eventually used the vine covered gazebo at the edge of Snowsoup stream for her wedding ceremony.)

The Bottom Line

So, here's what you can reasonably expect for the traditional wedding at someone else's casino, castle, or bed-and-breakfast:

The Small, Intimate, or "Informal" Wedding (15–25 guests)

Food and Drink $40/head=$1,000

You can easily go higher or lower, but keep in mind that you will easily save yourself a lot of money if you arrange the reception for lunchtime instead of dinnertime.

Facility Rental $1,000

That's what the experts say, but if you're on a tight budget, there are wonderful free or nearly free places—such as parks, beachfronts, your Aunt Betty's living room, or Uncle Morty's backyard.

Flowers $50–100 on up

Don't sweat the small stuff. Be a sport and get *a lot* of flowers.

Dress $250 on up (and up)
(Tuxedo=$100)

This is in parentheses because most men wouldn't choose to wear a tux for a small affair, but if you want to be really glitzy, just go ahead and do it. It's your wedding.

Photographer $500 on up

Videographer $1,500 on up

Don't let your cousin Kenny take the pictures, unless he's a professional photographer and he promises not to get drunk. Also, if you decide to get the whole shebang videotaped, don't let that same cousin Kenny do it under *any* circumstances. Videographers have no choice but to get in the way of everything—at some point you're going *(cont'd)* to trip over something and yell obscenities at them. Professionals are used to being bad-mouthed. Your cousin Kenny isn't. You don't want to cause a family rift, and you won't want the videotape.

Music (Deejay) $500 on up

As with the photographer: No Cousin Kenny. And keep in mind the quartet from Julliard may play for free in the subways, but they won't come cheap for your reception.

Cake $2 to $3/slice = $75

Bottom line:

I'd figure the whole affair for somewhere in the area of $3,500.

The Medium-Sized Arena Wedding
(100-plus guests)

Food and Drink (and facility): Dinner @ $50/head = $5,000. You can save considerably if you make it an early afternoon or Friday night affair. (Depending on the region, the price will be *at least* $50 per head.)

Liquor $2,000 (as opposed to drink)

Flowers $500 on up

As with the price per person, there is a tremendous variation in price by region (and by the willingness of the participants to take care of some of the facets of the process itself).

Dress $750 to $2,000 on up (and up)

Tuxedo $100 × the number of males in family plus the non-family ushers. (Often the groom's tux is free if you rent all the tuxedos from the same place.)

Photographer $1,500 on up (no cousin Kenny)

(cont'd)

Videographer $2000 on up

No Kenny, and no Uncle Murray who still owns the original six-ton Sharp video camera. Also, put the kibosh on your Godmother's nephew who's in film school at NYU. Don't scrimp on this. Scrimp (a little) on the next one:

Invitations $200

First, always remember George Castanza's experience with cheap invitations in *Seinfeld* (His fiance died from an allergic reaction to the glue on the ridiculously cheap invitations he ordered). Second, don't save $21.75 and get stationery that looks like you're inviting people to a theme birthday party. Third, don't spend a fortune on something that will be discarded and forgotten as soon as the RSVP card is returned. Despite what some people will tell you, wedding invitations are not high art. The calligraphy and the gold lettering and all that embossing may look nice for a second or two, but will definitely end up in the garbage along with the unopened Ed McMahon Publishers Clearinghouse envelopes and the banana peels. No one who is not institutionalized, except your mothers, will save your invitation. As Jon Kotcher of Cross Hair Graphics in New York City says, "It doesn't take a lot of money to make your invitation look elegant and stylish. And don't lose sight of the fact that the essential point of an invitation is to let people know when and where the affair is to take place."

Gifts for Bride's Attendants $150-plus

Nobody cares about these gifts as long as they don't look or come cheap. Then everybody cares.

Gifts for Groomsmen $125-plus or minus

Your groomsmen really don't care, but you still have to do it. So do it. But before you do it, see the section on Gifts for Groomsmen in Chapter 6.

Music (Deejay) $750 on up

Warning: This person is going to run your reception. (See Chapter 6.)

(cont'd)

Music (Band) $2,000 to $4500

Don't skimp if you go this route. (See Chapter 6.) You might think you've ended up on a cruise ship or at cousin Skippy's Bar Mitzvah.

Limousines $450 on up

Cake $3/slice=$300 on up

We received estimates from $250 to $1000. Look around before breaking the bank on this. The truth: nobody eats the cake. You just want it to look good. Check with our caterer or facility—cake may be included in your package.

Gift Baskets for Out-of-Town Guests $200

Personally, I think this is an unnecessary expense. The $15–20 knickknacks you get won't even begin to compensate the guests for their travel—and they may remind them that you're not paying for their hotel reservations. However, if your fiance or future mother-in-law insist, just smile and tack it on to the tab. It's not the place to draw any economic battle lines.

The Gonzo Wedding
(300 guests—or Just Puttin' on the Ritz)

The general prices for the medium-sized wedding apply here, you just have to do the multiplication to arrive at a reasonable figure for the size of your guest list. However, as they like to say in Hollywood, the sky is the limit on these affairs.

Joyce Smith, the president of Weddings Unlimited, Inc., in Cincinnati, reports online that she consulted for a $170,000 affair for 300 guests. The bare-bones expenses for the wedding (and keep in mind, we're talking Cincinnati) were:

Food and Beverages $300/head = $90,000

Flowers $30,000

(And I don't think we're talking about the Tuilleries in Paris.)

(cont'd)
- **Cake** $2,000

  (Given the other expenses, this sounds like a deal at approximately $6.50 a slice.)

- **Dress** $6,000

- **Photographer** $6,000

  (And they didn't get Ansel Adams or Annie Leibowitz.)

- **Music** $8,000

  (Two bands—one for cocktails and another for the reception. Not U2 or Tom Petty or P Diddy)

- **Wedding Consultant Fee** $5,000

  I don't begrudge Ms. Smith's fee—it's truly hard work planning a wedding. But keep in mind that $120,000 will buy a really terrific ring, a great honeymoon trip, a nice car, disease treatment, countless meals for starving people…and will still leave you with $50,000 to create one of the warmest and most enjoyable weddings for 300 of your closest friends that most anyone in Cincinnati has ever seen. And you can still do it for much less and still have a memorable time.

Financing the Affair (Gulp!)

What if you decide to pay for the big *I Do* yourselves? Good for you. That certainly helps to clear the driving lane. However, as is commonly understood, money is the number-one cause of marital discord throughout the long and winding *'til death do you part*, so please don't dig yourself a financial hole so deep in making your dream wedding a reality that the ensuing debt you take on will destroy your marriage.

(*Note:* This information is for you and your bride-to-be, not for your parents and your in-laws, unless they stumble upon it by themselves. If they want to pay for the wedding—and it's okay with the two of you—let them make their own financial arrangements. Even if you're a financial wizard, don't be their advisor—it has the possibility of making you look like a weasel. Simply thank them and then work with them.)

So, back to you: There are at least four strategies for financing the wedding of your dreams (if you can't pay for it out of pocket):

1. The pay-as-you-go plan.
2. Bridal loans.
3. Home equity loans.
4. Wedding sponsorships.

Pay-As-You-Go

Pay-as-you-go is simply another name for saving as much discretionary income as you possibly can in the weeks, months, and (God forbid!) years before the actual wedding. This also demonstrates the benefits of planning the wedding far enough in advance so that you can begin saving for it. This is clearly the best of all possible routes because it leaves you with the least possible debt.

Most wedding vendors—including caterers, reception facilities, florists, photographers, etc.—require a 50-percent deposit when hiring their services. According to Stacy Sheeley, CPA and financial Planner, systematic savings provide the best hedge against damaging debt. The more money you have to put down, the less you'll be in debt. Very simple.

Bridal Loans

Of course, the pay-as-you-go plan is much easier said than done. If that is particularly true in your case—and you still want to float a big number for the big game—getting a wedding loan, then, is probably your next best plan. Any number of institutions, including your own families' and banks you never heard of are available to underwrite the part of your dreams. MBNA America Bank, for example, offers wedding loans up to $25,000 for couples whose income and credit levels are acceptable. Check first with the bank where you normally do your business, but you can figure somewhere in the neighborhood of 13-percent or more interest with six or fewer years to pay.

Ms. Sheeley says to make sure there are no annual fees and no prepayment penalties. She also advises you to avoid the temptation to put the whole affair on a credit card (even if you're getting miles). It could end up costing you 20 percent or more in the long run.

Home Equity Loans

This is a slippery slope, warns Ms. Sheeley. Home equity loans (if you own your own home) and retirement plans will provide good sources of capital, but buyers should be wary.

Retirement plans are costly because they often create a "taxable event," plus a penalty for early withdrawal (unless you're 59 1/2 and probably not reading this anyway). Keep in mind, too, that although retirement seems a long way off now, your wedding will only last one day and retirement might indeed go on for several decades. You're gonna need that dough.

"Home equity loans or lines of credit," says Sheeley, "are the preferable choice, if you're going to borrow. The rates are generally considerably lower than conventional loans and the interest is tax deductible." She also advises that lines of credit are somewhat preferable to standard home equity loans, if only because psychologically it's better to not have the entire lump sum in your pocket right away. If it's there, you're going to spend it.

Wedding Sponsorships

This is a rather new and interesting wrinkle on how to pay for your wedding. It's similar to the practice of big businesses buying the rights to the names of public facilities and events all over America—only far more personal. Closer to home, it's similar to agreeing to get your car "wrapped" in advertisements in exchange for various services—or even getting a free car with a total wrap job.

The upside of sponsorships is that it makes it possible for you to obtain the kind of wedding you or your bride really really really want without mortgaging your entire future. Couples strapped for cash—or equity—can now barter with various wedding vendors for free or discounted services in exchange for various forms of advertising at the reception.

The bakery might, for example, reduce or even eliminate the cost of the wedding cake if you agree to put its name in the program or on a tasteful sign near the cutting table. The same goes for the music provider, the florist, the photographer, etc. As you might imagine, though, it's best to not ask the clergy for a discount.

Keep in mind, too, that some of your guests will consider sponsorships tacky. Those guests don't count, though. Only you and your bride can decide what is best or appropriate for your wedding day.

The downside to sponsorships generally involves two issues. The first, the more practical, concerns how labor intensive these arrangements can be. They are a lot more complicated to set up than conventional work-for-hire deals and because they are, in effect, partnerships, you will lose a percentage of control over the proceedings. That means you're going to do more negotiating than you might have imagined—or that you'd ever do if you were the one buying—and then demanding—their services.

The second drawback is more spiritual in nature. We live in a society where practically everything is for sale. That may or may not be okay for you as a general principle, but it is very important to consider when thinking about whether or not you want to turn one of the most intimate landmarks of your life into a marketing event. In essence, how much of your personal and private life is for sale?

Please keep this in mind: Despite what your father may or may not say about money not growing on trees, money should NOT be the driving force behind this event. Within reason, you certainly don't need a lot of money to have a beautiful day and, also within reason, you shouldn't let money stand in the way of your vision of what it takes to make it a beautiful day. No matter what, you will have a memorable time no matter how much you spend on this wedding. It's your day and your day alone—and hopefully it will be the only one you two ever know this intimately until your daughter hits you with her best shot.

And finally, this whole affair is more important than we often understand or acknowledge to the people whom we care most about. Don't denounce, dismiss, or denigrate the whole wedding thing as if it's a waste of money or time. And above all, don't whine about it. Whining might have been effective with your mother way back when, but it won't work with your fiance—and absolutely no man looks cute or manly when he's pouting. If it's very important to your fiance, it's very important—and even more important that you treat it that way. Smile all the way to the bank.

Chapter 8

The Xs and Os

Put it any way you want—nuts and bolts, Xs and Os, Ps and Qs, the nitty gritty, dollars and cents, the bottom line—and it all pretty much comes down to the same thing: hunkering down to do what you need to do to make your lifetime partnership work. (This may also be known as "What you will need to know if everything doesn't go exactly according to Plan A, which is 'Get engaged, get married, live happily ever after.'")

After all the candy and the flowers and the sweet words and the moonlit nights and the shimmering diamonds, there's some real-world accounting to be done—some of it before you're married, the rest of it after. As an equal partner in this lifelong enterprise, you will not only want to be knowledgeable and conversant with a wide range of financial and legal topics related to a solvent marriage, but your new millennium bride will undoubtedly expect you to carry your own weight in the business of your forthcoming marriage. That's it.

In her most interesting book on the strikingly different ways that men and women communicate (or fail to communicate), *You Just Don't Understand* (Quill, 2001), Deborah Tannen talks rather convincingly of the different conversation styles of men and women. Basically, men use language to establish hierarchy while women speak to develop connections. That helps to explain why men and women so often misunderstand each other. It also helps us to understand the male unwillingness to ask for—or follow—directions. None of us males want to be anything less than the alpha monkey. As much as it pains me to admit that all those female stand-up comedians and silly sitcom jokes are correct, on this particular point they all seem to be right on the money. In general, men don't like to follow directions, whether it's coming from gas station attendants, our mothers, our girlfriends, our fathers, or the miserably written step-by-step instructions from the Weber Grill Corporation. (Note: We do manage to take directions from bosses and supervisors, but then only grudgingly.) Partially, I suspect, it's a matter of pride in our independent know-how; and partially it's an expression of our innate understanding of how men learn best. Either way, we don't like much about instructions, unless, of course, we're giving them.

Nevertheless, the most important thing that all of us learn at one point or another about becoming men is that we just have to suck it up sometimes and listen to someone who knows more about the subject than we do. And ultimately—please trust me on this point—this stuff is as important as the hearts and flowers and jewelry, and it's going to make you feel more in control of your destiny. Once you feel more in control of your destiny, you'll be far less likely to have to listen to anyone else's advice anytime soon.

With all that in mind, I'm going to make this as brief and straightforward as possible. No jokes, no cute takes, and no sports metaphors—just some very basic issues that should be addressed by every groom-to-be who aims to be the very good husband and father his bride dreams of him being.

There are two pillars upon which a healthy marriage rests: financial and legal.

Pillar 1: The Financial Xs

As a card carrying member of the Woodstock generation, I (and most of my friends) once regarded financial planning as the work of the establishment devil. That was not only an indication of our charming arrogance as a generation, but as a sign of our abject ignorance of one of the pillars of a successful union. (This is another reason why so many of my friends are divorced.)

It is by now common knowledge that more than 50 percent of all marriages end in divorce. It is also common knowledge that money problems constitute the number one cause of divorce in this country.

Despite the fact that we love the myth of love transcending money in this culture, experience demonstrates that money has the ability to trump good humor, good sex, good food, and even good companionship. And as we understand from Abraham Maslow, if you don't have your financial house in order, then your marriage is in real danger of falling down. Thus, it is in your best interest to understand how to nourish and protect your financial well-being.

Ruth L. Hayden, an internationally known financial consultant from St. Paul, Minnesota, and the author of a wonderfully helpful book on money management, *For Richer, Not Poorer: The Money Book for Couples* (Health Communications, 1999), says that the problem is not money itself. "Poor money gets beat up. The truth is that nobody is disagreeing on how much $100 is worth. What the couples are disagreeing about is what they should do...and how to talk about it."

With that in mind, I found it very interesting that in interviews with several attorneys, who admittedly are not involved in the psychodynamics of an unhappy home, the immediate cause of divorce is rarely money itself. Andrew Kossover, a New Paltz, New York, attorney and lecturer who has been practicing litigation law—with an emphasis in matrimonial and family law—since 1977, told me that most people coming to his office are seeking divorces because their spouses are having affairs. In truth, money problems may be an integral factor in leading one partner to have an affair, but it is the affair itself that gives the other partner motivation to leave the marriage.

Hayden says a couple can head off all sorts of problems by learning how to talk about money. "Despite the fact that money is the primary motivator for fighting and estrangement in marriage, there is no place in this society where couples learn to talk about money," she explains. "It is still taboo. In fact, couples would rather talk about their sex life than money. As a result most couples lack the management tools to keep their relationship on an even keel."

Over many generations, couples have been taught that there are three ways to manage money:

1. Both fight.
2. One is supposed to acquiesce.
3. Both remain silent.

Your Dreamboat Is Not Your Financial Clone

Hayden says that the first thing to understand is that just as your relationship develops and evolves over time, so do your expectations about what it means to be a good and loving partner. "On that first date, we're all intrigued by differences. Then after we've been going out for a while and make a commitment, everything changes. Then we want that person to think and behave like we do—like a clone. What once felt intriguing now feels wrong."

Yet everyone knows (don't you? please say yes) that even though some part of you really wants her to go along with everything you say, it would eventually prove to be hell on earth. The very last thing you really want or need in a partner is a clone.

The second thing to understand according to Hayden is that the "emotional drives the rational parts of our lives (and they're not bi-lingual)." That's why it is so helpful for engaged couples to break away from all the deliriously wonderful romance for a few moments before they tie the knot. They need to have a dialogue about the ways in which they hope to conduct their lives, given their resources. "It will make them light years ahead of other couples." Further, it will help set a standard for Hayden's suggestion of weekly money meetings once they are married (see Chapter 15).

Hayden advises to begin the process by trying to understand the differences between financial beliefs (emotional) and financial behavior (rational). "Belief statements always involve *should*—no facts, not a right answer—and 98 percent of money statements are belief statements." An example is: "No one should spend more than $100 on a meal." That's a belief. In practice, many people can and do spend that kind of money at a restaurant and do not see any moral or ethical sins taking place. A behavior statement is more along the lines of: "We don't make enough money to afford to spend $100 on a meal." That's a fact. If it's not in your wallet, you don't have it. Facts have to do with diversification and dollar cost averaging. "Anything more than that slides into emotions and that's where I find that most couples stumble."

That's why you need to separate belief and behavior to get to the data you need to enhance your lives. For example, is college education important for yourselves or your children—or is an annual vacation to the beach a necessity for a good life? Both of these are common beliefs.

However, if both of you agree on the merits of one belief or another, then you can move on to the level of behavior; that is, how much money from each paycheck should we be putting into a college fund or an annual vacation account?

Hayden asserts that although women are supposed to be more emotional than men, she finds that when it comes to money, most men have a harder time separating emotions and data. At the heart of that disparity is the widely held belief in our culture that men are supposed to be good providers and good at money—and that they should know how to manage a family's finances by virtue of their genetic material. That's a lot of pressure.

The First Financial Summit

In that first financial meeting, both of you need to lay your financial cards on the table. It is just as important to not pass any judgments about the way you or your partner has managed your money. Hayden says "If you're willing to have an open dialogue—if you're willing to learn to talk—if you're willing to not always have to be right—then money is just a tool to make your values work toward your goals."

First, each of you should make a short list concerning a few very solid facts about your economic position:

1. How much money does each of us make?
2. How much money does each of us take home?
3. What are our regular monthly expenses?
4. How much debt does each of us carry (credit cards, college loans, car loans, etc.)?
5. How much equity does each of us hold (trusts, real estate, investments, etc.)?
6. What are the realistic prospects for either or both of us losing, maintaining, or increasing income in the near future?

Once you know where both of you stand, you can begin the belief dialogue and start the process of sharing beliefs and turning them into shared behavior. For example, what are your long- and short-term financial goals? How much debt is acceptable? How much debt can you reasonably handle? Under what circumstances will you use your credit card(s)? How much money should each of you be putting away from your paycheck toward the last 30 years of your life together?

The Checkbook Questions

This is a real nuts and bolts issue that can be handled in that first prenuptial meeting. It goes right to the heart of how you are going to handle your money as a couple. At one end of the spectrum are couples that handle everything jointly; that is, all their earnings go into joint checking and savings accounts, and all their bills get paid out of those same joint accounts. Way at the other end of the spectrum are the couples who have separate accounts for everything; that is, each of them pays an agreed upon portion of all household expenses from his or her own private account.

Neither way is necessarily right or wrong says Hayden. "The only wrong thing is not to discuss it." However, she adds that the way that you handle your money "...should look like the relationship itself. If a couple is totally enmeshed—then everything is 'yours, mine, and ours.' If the two of you are more independent in spirit and practice—then the finances should look more like 'ours and mine.' The critical factors are to make sure that both of you are happy with the arrangement and that each of your 'books' is open to the other's scrutiny."

Hayden concludes by saying, "Compromise is an essential skill in household money management. When you get to the point of realizing that you're not losing—you are stretching—then the system is in place, and both of you should feel relieved." She adds, "Both of you should feel a little uncomfortable. If not, someone is not stretching. But if the numbers work and it feels fair, uncomfortable but fair, then they have a heck of a system."

Plan for Autonomy Money

Whatever financial set-up you decide upon, though, what Hayden calls "autonomy money" is absolutely necessary to the well-being of your financial relationship. "Couples need to trust each other to have independent money. Assume core trust. That is, 'You're not going to spend money that will hurt us in any way—and neither am I.' Rather than one partner sneaking around behind the other's back to buy things he or she wants, which happens all too often (and has been going on for all too many years) there must be some money for which neither partner has to be accountable—coins in the pocket or running money."

Then the question becomes one of dollars and cents, which is manageable. How much running money can we afford? Does one of us need more running money than the other? Why? How will the autonomy money get distributed and how often?

Does the System Work?

Does the system work? That's a great question and one that should be asked and answered on a regular basis, but it's also a question that probably won't be answered until quite a while after you've been married. You need to live with the joint or separate accounts for a while. You need to see how much autonomy money you really need. You need to see how your debt load is changing over time.

That said, taking your financial temperature should be a regular activity for newlyweds. That's why Hayden's idea of weekly money meetings is so important (see Chapter 15). It's the only way for a young and busy couple to stay on top of their financial well-being. As couples grow together and their lives become more complicated (with mortgages, children, vacation homes, dogs, etc.), the finances become increasingly complicated as well. But the criteria for whether the system works is always the same:

1. Are we able to pay our bills?
2. Does it feel fair?

Should You Get Insurance?

Whether you're 22, 32, or 92 years old and about to get married for the first—or the 17th—time, you need to a good grasp of why insurance is so important to ensure future happiness . After all, marriage is for richer or poorer, in sickness and in health.

My experts all agree—you need insurance once you're hitched. Ruth L. Hayden suggests that you spend a little time at that first financial discussion talking about insurance. "It's easier to talk about unfortunate eventualities such as loss, disease, and death while you're still madly in love and want to do everything you can do in your power to protect each other."

She says that you need health, life, and disability insurance. Mr. Andrew Kossover adds that if you're renting a home or apartment, you need renters insurance. "It's not just about you and your things anymore," he explains. "You have an obligation to protect community property." And, of course, you need—desperately need—a health insurance policy that will protect your loved ones and keep the family from the poorhouse after the first medical crisis.

Granted, it is probably more difficult to see the logic in spending your hard-earned money on catastrophic health insurance when you're in your 20s and 30s and in the bloom of excellent health. Yet, just as one needs automobile insurance for all the unforeseen—and often unimagined—accidents both major and minor, that afflict everyone, regardless of age, money, class, driving record, or devotion to God and country, each responsible adult in a marriage needs protection in the form of health insurance, life insurance, income insurance, and domicile insurance.

Home or Renters Insurance

This is fairly straightforward. Begin with the notion that, even if you never thought of insurance before, you now owe it to your spouse, if not yourself, to protect those assets from fire, theft, wind, water, etc. As a happy-go-lucky bachelor you might have considered your possessions as essentially "easy come–easy go." After all, they're just things. However, when your things (or her things) become our things, then you owe it to each other to protect one another from loss.

Then you will need to make a list of your assets. Keep in mind that your net worth may increase significantly as a result of all the wedding presents you are going to be receiving, so you might want to wait until after the wedding before setting up a renters policy or, if you already own a house or condominium, amending the present policy. In any case, no married couple should be without a home policy of one type or another.

Health Insurance

Health insurance is a no-brainer. Everybody needs one form of health insurance or another. Hopefully, your employer—or hers— already provides a type of coverage that will protect both of you. If not, you have hopefully already made arrangements for health insurance on your own that can, if necessary, be amended to include coverage for your spouse. And if not, you need to take care of that right away—before you are married.

As with home insurance, the essential fact is that it's not about just you anymore. Unexpected serious injuries or major illnesses (after all, all injuries and illnesses are unexpected), can not only decimate your holdings, but prevent you from making a decent living in the future. You need to protect her in case you're no longer able to provide for—and protect—her financial health in the future. And just so the record is straight: She owes the very same to you.

Disability Insurance

Another no-brainer: If you're dependent on income, you need disability insurance. As previously mentioned, it would be nice if your employer took care of this kind of insurance. But if not, you owe it to your spouse to protect her when you are no longer able to provide for her. (As she does owe you.)

Life Insurance

No one likes to think about the death of a spouse, but it must be considered if the two of you are going to be fair with each other. Hayden suggests that all couples need straight life insurance. That is, you pay a monthly premium with no return unless one of you dies. "The only ones who believe in investment or whole life policies are insurers," she says. Whatever you decide, however, the core reason to have life insurance to is give the survivor a buffer—a full year—to regroup after the death.

"For a lot of couples carrying enough insurance enough to pay off the house is sufficient. Others—especially those with dependents or those where one partner earns most of the income for the household—will need considerably more."

She adds, "If you have a financial plan and it's working, then you'll essentially be self-insured (and can drop insurance)."

Pillar 2: The Law and the Married Guy

The second pillar of a happy, healthy marriage involves a basic understanding of laws that affect your engagement and marriage, and the ways in which they intersect with the unwritten rules of your own relationship.

Andrew Kossover clarifies the nuts and bolts issues facing couples about to get married. Kossover reminds us of the important distinction between what is right and what is legal, what you should do and what you are required by law to do. He also reminds us that the law protects us best when things are going the worst. When you're head over heels in love, you have a lot of trouble conceptualizing or planning for trouble. But the truth is that nobody's life is trouble free and it is in your best interest to wedding protocol as well as problem protocol.

So, Who Owns the Rock if the Game Goes South?

You bought that beautiful diamond ring with your hard-earned money (or your well-worn credit card) so you might naturally think it is yours, even though she's wearing it. She, on the other hand, might believe that the rock that was given to her is more than a ring, it is evidence of a formal offer to marry her—and by virtue of her allowing it to be slipped on her finger, she is in good faith agreeing to the deal. She may believe that once the band passes the knuckle, it's a sealed contract, and no matter what happens to either of you, it's hers.

Well, as John Mellencamp once told us, "it doesn't matter what you think, you can't fight the law. The law always wins." And here's the law (for any of you budding lawyers out there, Kossover says this question comes up on virtually every bar exam): Under the broad umbrella of NYS Civil Rights Law (Sec. 80b), the engagement ring question is known as the Heart Balm Statute. That is, the engagement ring represents a gift given in contemplation of an event. And that means that if either party cancels the wedding, the ring remains the property of the giver. Given in contemplation of an event that no longer has an expectation of taking place, he retains rights to the ring and the property reverts to the buyer. Kossover says he has had several clients who have gone through legal challenges to get back the rings they bought for their ex-fiances—and in the process he had to have the rings evaluated by diamond experts to certify that the stone that was given is the same stone that was returned.

However, once the formal "I do's" are done—and the names are signed on the dotted line, the ring is hers, forever and ever. Even if the marriage breaks up in a day (or a year, or 20 years, or the later part of a lifetime), the ring will always be hers. Cut your losses and go.

What About Wedding Bills and Cold Feet?

Okay, so what happens if you get cold feet—or it turns out that your honey is having her feet warmed and toes curled by some other Adonis—before the two of you actually make it to the altar?

And what if she (or her family) has already forked over thousands upon thousands of down-payment dollars to caterers, photographers, limo companies, etc. and have no way of recouping their funds? Are you liable for the costs incurred by the bride's family in planning your wedding?

Kossover says this is simple general contract law. "Legally, no. Unless the groom-to-be obligated himself to the vendors, there is no legal requirement to share in the losses."

That said, Kossover emphatically reminds future grooms that there remains a moral or ethical obligation to pay for at least one half of the lost deposits. It comes down to a question of character. No matter what has gone down, no matter who is calling off the wedding, this is clear: both of you agreed to get married in a certain manner, and each of you proceeded in good faith on that agreement. You may not be legally liable, but you bear responsibility, especially if you are calling off the event.

What About Being Jilted?

As you know or might well imagine, being left at the altar—or dumped late in the engagement—is particularly painful and humiliating. Yet, according to Kossover, contractual suits from jilted brides are pretty much a dead end. Even if you signed some kind of promissory document guaranteeing your faithful participation in the wedding, she would have to prove that you were a cad, intentionally inflicting harm by your non-appearance and that would be very difficult.

Prenuptial Agreements

First, despite the fact that prenups are now an integral part of the language of marriage (they're all over TV and movies), I suspect that most people don't really understand what a prenup is or what it is designed to do.

So, what is a prenup? A prenuptial agreement is a private agreement between a prospective bride and groom in which the two agree upon the disposition of their property in the event of death or divorce. It is designed to override or clarify the law that otherwise would apply. Simple enough...or is it?

Arlene J. Dubin, the author of *Prenups for Lovers: A Romantic Guide to Prenuptial Agreements* (Villard Books, 2001) and partner at Rubin-Baum LLP where she specializes in matrimonial law, is a staunch proponent of prenuptial agreements. She asserts that upwards of 20 percent of all marriages today are preceded by prenups—and that by 2020 she expects that 50 percent will be effectively prenupted.

In her very helpful book on prenups, Ms. Dubin has outlined 24 reasons to engage in a prenup, but in a recent exclusive interview she identified the two primary reasons for such a legal agreement: "The number one reason [to establish a prenup] is that the divorce rate in our country is almost 50 percent. Another reason is that the divorce laws in our country are subjective, and judges have a great deal of discretion." She also mentions the facts that (a) the median duration for a first marriage that ends in divorce is 6.3 years (which is not a really long time) and (b) 75 percent of people who divorce will eventually remarry (which is a lot of people). The combination of those two facts suggests that it is not only wise to consider a prenup, it is prudent.

An Interview With Arlene Dubin on Prenups

Steve: Do you recommend that all couples arrange a prenup? Are there any situations where you think a prenup is not necessary or even advisable?

Arlene: I think that all couples should at least consider a prenuptial agreement. They should educate themselves in the marital and probate laws that otherwise would apply to them without an agreement. They should inform each other fully of their assets, liabilities, income, and prospective gifts and inheritance. Then they should decide if they want to write the rules that will govern their relationship or be governed by the default law. Even if a couple doesn't actually execute a prenuptial, they will benefit from the education and communication that results from the process.

Steve: Are prenups more important for some groups than others (such as wealthier couples or second marriages)?

Arlene: The traditional customer for a prenuptial agreement is the older, more mature couple, with substantial assets and children from a prior marriage to protect. Although it is vital for this customer to have a prenuptial agreement, today we see more and more demand from young people entering into first marriages. Younger people are marrying later than ever before, and by the time that they do, they often have some assets (a car, a home, stock options, or a 40l(k) plan). Even if they don't have assets, they often have debts, especially student loans or credit card bills. It is vital to disclose these debts to a partner and determine how they will be paid off. If a young person doesn't have assets or debts, he/she often has prospects (that is, a degree, a small business, or a budding career). In addition, young people are inheriting money—$50 trillion is being passed down in the next five decades in the greatest intergenerational transfer of wealth in history.

Steve: It's easy to understand why the wealthier partner gains through a prenup. However, what benefits, if any, does the less wealthy partner accrue by signing a prenuptial agreement?

Arlene: Prenups can be used proactively by the less-wealthy individual to make sure that he or she gets his or her fair share of the assets. Individuals who relocate, take a part-time job, sacrifice a career to take care of the home and family, or put a spouse through school can use a prenuptial to make sure that they are compensated for their contributions to the marriage.

Steve: Do prenups only pertain to property or are there other "assets" (children, sperm/eggs, pets, creative ideas, business plans, names, etc.) that can be included in the agreement?

Arlene: There is a growing demand today for inclusion of "lifestyle" issues in the prenuptial, such as bad boy/bad girl clauses which punish bad behavior such as cheating, overeating, drinking, and the like. My recommendation is to discuss all of your issues, but I would suggest limiting the prenuptial to the property issues. Although the property clauses are legally enforceable, the lifestyle clauses are only morally persuasive. Usually they are too vague to be enforced, and their inclusion in a prenuptial might taint the enforceability of the property issues.

Steve: Is a living will an appropriate part of a prenup?

Arlene: This is not usually done in a prenuptial. There is no presumptive right of a spouse to be designated. (My translation: do a living will, but not as part of prenup.)

Steve: On the Right on the Money Website (*rightonthemoney.com*), you are quoted as saying that "prenups should be addressed as early as possible, but no later than a public engagement. I recommend that you discuss the topic generally, even while you're dating." I think most of us understand why it's preferable to broach the subject earlier than later, but I also suspect most men (and women) are thinking with their hearts, not their heads, during their courtships and, as such, their assets are not on the radar. What do you say to those who assert that prenups take the romance out of the romance?

Arlene: Prenups stimulate communication and compromise. When people start to talk about the big bugaboo—money—they tend to open up about personal issues. The dialogue strengthens the emotional bond between people. Economic intimacy leads to emotional intimacy. When people put their money issues behind them, they clear the air and continue romantically. A relationship that is grounded in reality has a greater chance for happily-ever-after than one based on illusion. And what's so romantic about a messy divorce?

Steve: Are online or do-it-yourself prenups adequate or do you recommend always using an attorney? Can any attorney set up a prenup or is it advisable to engage the services of a lawyer specifically experienced in the field? Should the future bride and groom each have an attorney to review the agreement?

Arlene: Each party should hire his or her separate, independent lawyer. My book is a how-to-do-it book, and why-to-do-it book, but not a do-it-yourself. You should hire an attorney experienced in prenuptial agreements. These are usually trusts and estates or matrimonial lawyers. You should look for a lawyer who is a negotiator, because the objective of a prenuptial agreement is to work out an agreement that is fair and balanced; both parties must derive a benefit so the process is not about "winning."

(*Note:* With respect to Ms. Dubin, there is some disagreement over whether it is necessary to hire an attorney for your prenup. If you are interested in reviewing a sample do-it-yourself prenup, you can find a good one at *prenupKit.com*. If you decide to go with a lawyer, it will help you understand the process a little better. If you decide to go it alone, then it will provide a simple and easy to follow roadmap to legal and financial protections in marriage.)

Steve: If one engages an attorney, what can he or she reasonably expects the fees to be?

Arlene: Prenups can cost in a range of a few hundred dollars to tens of thousands of dollars, depending upon complexity.

Steve: Can prenups be amended over time or are couples essentially "stuck" with the agreement they signed before they got married?

Arlene: Prenups can and should be amended after marriage if there is a change in circumstances.

One Reason *Not* to Do a Prenup

Andrew Kossover has a slightly different take on the question of whether to create a prenup or not. He says that after handling hundreds of divorce cases, he has come to the conclusion that in his estimation there is one compelling reason to consider *not* having a prenup. "It really does take away from the romance, if only momentarily. You have to deal with that." I might add that real life—everyday life—tends to take away a little of the romance out of romance. Yet, at a time when couples are swept up in that giddy emotional high in anticipation of living happily ever after, having to think about money, divorce, death, and other decidedly undreamy subjects rains on the parade.

Kossover explains that if both parties are entering marriage on a "level playing field" (that is, their net worth is about the same)—another compelling reason to have the lay-your-cards-on-the-table financial discussion during your engagement—there is probably no compelling reason to write a prenup. Nevertheless, he counsels that all engaged couples "be honest with each other. Take a minute out of the romance to talk about your financial status—and your expectations for sharing the wealth. Then you'll know whether or not a prenup is really necessary.

"You also have to check how your home states regard assets in divorce," Kossover adds. For example, in New York there is what is known as Equitable Distribution; that is, husband and wife are considered economic partners in marriage—and in the case of divorce, money/support is awarded in context with how much time and sacrifice has gone into building the couple's assets. If husband and wife are married a long time and during the course of that marriage a certain amount of equity was built up, both partners are going to share as equitably as possible in the sale or ownership of that property. However, if most of the wealth was gained prior to the marriage—and the marriage itself did not last very long—then the distribution will be quite lopsided in favor of the wealthier partner.

In contrast, California considers all assets "community property" upon marriage, and thus, each partner immediately shares an equal standing in his or her mate's financial holdings (or debt). It doesn't matter how long you are married or how much you contributed to the profit or loss—it's half yours.

The bottom line: Find out what the deal is in your state. You can't play the game effectively if you don't understand the rules.

And what do you find at the bottom of the bottom line? Kossover says, "Caveat Emptor: Beware of who you get engaged to."

And I'd like to add: Know thyself.

Chapter 9

10 Taboos for the Bachelor Party

Let me be frank: This is a particularly challenging topic to do the usual Xs and Os. Bachelor parties are pure dynamite—both the kind that are, as skinny Jimmy Walker used to say on *Good Times* ("Dy-No-Mite!") and the kind that explode in your hand like grenades or errant cherry bombs.

Ancient tradition dictates that a man should have a good time in his final hours as a single man (in essence, as a boy). Indeed, there is evidence of pre-marital bacchanalia going on way back before ancient Greek men plighted their troth. Most everyone agrees that the groom-to-be should experience, for one final evening, the freedom to be as carefree and bad-breathed and unshaven and slackerly and poorly dressed as he ever was—and might never ever be again. He should bond with his boyhood friends (regardless of their age and standing in the community) before sharing his life—and his hopes and dreams—with a girl who will ostensibly do everything in her power to transform that footloose boy into a man rooted in family. In capsule, he should taste the unmitigated pleasures of being the boy he will never outgrow, but will agree to send to domestic military school for the next several decades of his life.

That said, navigating a successful bachelor party is a bit like being a member of the social bomb squad. It's fun and dangerous and made even more fun because its danger. As everybody knows, boys having a good time being boys sometimes means doing the kinds of things that others (that is, girls) might consider in bad taste, or immoral, or even potentially illegal. At the very least, bachelor parties encourage the kind of behavior that is generally deemed wholly unacceptable for adults—and certainly unacceptable to the lady of your dreams. And because of the element of desperation—the last gasp of youth—and because bachelor parties are so inherently edgy and precarious, the whole thing is made even more fun than going out with the boys normally might be.

All of which could turn into one of the most memorable nights of your life—or into a deal breaker for the starry-eyed bride-to-be. Can you hear the hissing of the wick just before it reaches the explosive powder?

Riding the Pine

Of course, you can avoid all the landmines by opting out of the traditional "last game" altogether. You can, perhaps for the first time in your life, choose wisdom over appetite and, in effect, bench yourself and sit it out. Let your friends party for you. Let them drink too much, carouse too far, speak too loud, stay out too late, play the too cool fool. Stay home with your folks or visit your lonely grandmother or take the time be alone and ponder the profound changes that will go on in your life as soon as you do the I Do.

Opting out is, of course, the safest route to the altar. But please understand that playing it safe means that you'll be missing out on a signal cultural event that a lot of men think should be in everyone's scrapbook of memories. It also means that you will be a no-show at the only bachelor party you will—hopefully—ever have. And, as long as we're being honest, do keep in mind that if you choose the safe course, all your friends will spend the night into morning laughing behind your back (and snickering in your face) at how you've become the poster boy for whipped hubbies around the globe. In that event, you'll simply have to be content with the knowledge that you'll be able to count on having a wife to get married to the next day.

No Regrets

However, should you choose appetite over wisdom, the essential up-front message for this chapter is that you really (really really) don't want to participate in anything that you will regret the next day—or be reminded of every day for the next 50 years of your married life.

Regret is a numbing emotion that sucks the joy out of the most pleasurable experiences and, more often than not, robs us of the ability to be fully present in our lives. It makes us question almost everything we do.

Beware the Best Man—or the Jealous Brother

Please note that in masterminding your own bachelor party, you have to be extra alert because your best man and your brothers and the groomsmen and practically any other male invited to your bachelor party will see it as their male duty to make you step over every moral and ethical and romantic line ever devised in the history of civilization. It's not totally clear why this is so, but your brothers-in-arms want you drunk, broke, debauched, smelly, and essentially unfit for the altar.

It's hard to figure out the complex motivations behind trying to ruin your wedding day, but perhaps they think that in protecting you from the claws and fangs of the woman who has you in her grasp—and who is going to civilize you to the point that you're no longer recognizable in male company—they feel they are somehow protecting themselves from such fate. Who knows? Nevertheless, please be aware that your lifelong friends might not always *be* your friends on the appointed day.

The 10 Taboos for the Bachelor Party

Okay, so here we go...these are the 10 absolute taboos that you must avoid during your final night of freedom:

1. **No prostitutes**. This should be a no-brainer, but there are legions of men who have walked the path before you who have breached this noble number-one hard-and-fast rule—and some have barely lived to regret it. Thus, it needs at least a brief mention. Whatever lame rationalizations you come up with (I'll never sleep with another woman for the rest of my life...I have never slept with anyone—or anyone besides my fiance—and it is my duty now to protect her from my wandering eye down the road apiece) or pathetic excuses you come up with ex-post facto (I was drunk...it didn't mean anything...I was so

nervous about the wedding that I didn't know what I was doing...my friends set me up...my friends drugged me...), you need to terminate this ancient activity immediately and with severe prejudice. Don't even think about it. Aside from the usual admonitions about STDs, AIDS/HIV, and moral character, messing with a prostitute will be viewed as the ultimate betrayal of your beloved—by your beloved. You may be confident that it would be meaningless fun, that men can have sex without getting emotionally involved, but your betrothed simply cannot help but be emotionally involved in you having sex with anyone else but her. Besides, I suspect the jury's still out on whether or not men can really divorce sex and love—or at least affection.

2. **Not even lap dancing.** The controlling sexual axiom for engaged and married men is simply "Look But Don't Touch—Or Be Touched" and there's no way that any kind of lap dance (except the one you're watching on video) does not involve touching. Although I've heard lap dancing described as a kind of "near beer," it is nothing of the sort. It is beer, and as such it is inebriating. And there's nothing quite like an inebriated man in the company of a naked woman rubbing up against him to enable him to forget the reason he was going to his bachelor party in the first place. Besides, there's not a bride in existence who doesn't understand the difference between watching naked ladies on a stage and what's going on when another woman is dancing on her man's lap. She is not going to be happy about it—ever. And here's another thing: The truth is that most men do not own a good set of brakes when the engine is red lining and the wheels are spinning almost out of control. In other words, when you're driving to the basket for a slam dunk, there's not much short of Shaquille O'Neal in the lane that can stop you. And that's who your sweet fiance is going to look like when you run into her after a night of drinking and lap dancing.

3. **No drinking til you puke** (especially if the party is the night before the wedding). I know this one may come as

10 Taboos for the Bachelor Party 127

a bit of a surprise, but barfing in public is disgusting. And I know that you've been doing this since at least your freshman year in college—and probably years before then. But you should know this: Everyone thinks that puking is revolting, except maybe your friends who are ralfing next to you or laughing at you upchucking on your own feet. Plus, hungover grooms with green faces and slack jaws and nasty breath mess up every wedding photograph in the album. And, strictly from a father's point of view, do not forget about the salient fact that a few years down the road you're going to have to explain to your own teenagers why it was okay for you to be a jackass on the night before your wedding, but they have to be alcohol free.

4. **No stealing stuff.** I'm not talking banks or convenient stores or grand theft auto or mugging old ladies. This one falls right into the harmless "boys will be boys" or "one last time for old glory" category. You know, like street signs...beer out of the neighbor's garage...dining and dashing...one last Playboy from the neighborhood convenience store...all for old times' sake. As I said, this is generally pretty harmless stuff, but on the off-chance that some rookie cop (or an old and bitter cop who hates rookies, his ex-wife, and anyone whose life is on the upswing) collars you with a Yield sign in the back seat of the car or nabs you racing out of the Olive Garden with check in hand and giggling like drunk hyenas, you're going to have a hard time explaining to your fiance (not to mention her mother, her father, *your* mother, and *your father*!) why you need to be bailed out of jail on the evening of your wedding.

5. **No gambling with your wedding money.** A lot of grooms-to-be hold their bachelor parties at casinos. And casinos, by and large, big and small, actually make a great choice for these affairs because practically everything you'll ever need for an A-1 last gasp extravaganza is found under one roof. (This includes the bonus that no one has to be a designated driver—and you won't have to worry about losing the deposit on the limo.) At the casino you can do

what you're going to do in a place where everyone is pretty much doing the same thing (wedding plans or not) and then sleep it off in a clean bed, arriving at the ceremony clear-eyed, refreshed and ready to step it up a notch. The problem is gambling is a lot like sex: Once you get going, it takes a bigger man than most of us to put on the brakes. Plus, once you're on a good roll, any man worth his salt can make the most manly of justifications concerning the future well-being of his wife (and children) if he could just put it all on red 14. Plus, you're going to be feeling a little more flush than usual with all the wedding cash flowing in. That's why everyone tells everyone else to go to casinos with only the amount of cash they are willing to lose. Everyone knows the virtue of leaving the credit cards at home. Yet, despite all the warnings, there are more bankrupt bettors than there are lights on the Vegas strip. So be vigilant—and please keep in mind that the problem is compounded maybe 100-fold by the fact that you know that you're going to get a bundle of cash for your wedding. After a few drinks (which almost every casino gives you gratis for just this reason), when you are still capable of basic arithmetical functions, you might even consider it your duty to double or triple it for the down payment on the house of her dreams, or the boat of yours, or just to finally pay off those college loans. As country singer Kenny Rogers once warned us, you "got to know when to hold 'em, know when to fold 'em." Be vigilant.

6. **No calling ex-girlfriends.** This is not as uncommon as you might think. Although we men are supposed to be stoic, unemotional types, in the right circumstances we can be as sentimental as any woman. And the right circumstances usually involve either underdogs' triumphing or the end of boyhood—almost every man alive gets teary when he hears "Oh Danny Boy" or when he sees the movie *Rudy* for the 15th time. And because getting married is the ultimate end of childhood and underdog achieving (we all think we're dogs unworthy of the women who chose us), most of us get pretty emotional, blubbering

in our beers, during the days before we get betrothed. Because we can't talk to our friends about our fears—and we certainly can't talk to our fiances about them—some men almost instinctively turn to an old girlfriend to cry on her shoulder. You may think that she's a safe bet because, first of all, she's already seen you at your worst, which is probably why you broke up in the first place, and second, regardless of how much she hates you, she loves it that you're choosing her to be "real" with instead of her replacement. Very dangerous. *Very, very dangerous.* In your mind, paint her door with lamb's blood so the avenging angel will pass by. You could find yourself crying on her shoulder, a picture which, however innocent it may have been, will make you look very guilty if the news gets back to your fiance.

7. **No brawling.** This is just like the puking admonition. No one, absolutely no one, except the aforementioned single friends and fraternity brothers (and maybe your brothers) will think better of you if you get into a bar fight the night before you get married. Think black eyes and missing teeth in photographs. Think jail. Think about the scowl on your bride's face. Reverse the order of the "getting bailed out" scenario: Think about the scowl on your mother-in-law's face

8. **No videos.** Go out, do some things that bring you right to the edge, be nasty, have a good time, even have a great time…but don't leave a video record of any of it behind. The video tape will haunt you all your remaining days. No one—except someone who would like to undermine the rest of your happily married life—wants to see you dancing on a bar with your boxers around your ankles. No one wants to see you with a tube down your throat, quarters in your crack, or kissing your best friend. If you must, bring along a throwaway camera, take pictures of everything, then throw away all the really nasty shots along with all the nasty negatives.

9. **No crying.** Your bachelor party is more than just fun. It is more than a big night on the town. It is, in truth, a deeply emotional, heavily symbolic event that marks the

very end of a man's boyhood. And, as such, it is wrought with deep, previously unexpressed feelings. So, this is for those of you who wear your emotions on your sleeve (generally not a bad quality, by the way): Please remember how hard you laughed—and how much disdain was in your voice—when one of your good buddies dissolved into a teary sentimental mess over the "bond" he feels with his old friends. Go to the mirror and make your crying face. Don't take a picture of it, but think about the throwaway camera and your crying mug being posted on the Internet.

10. **No "good boy parties."** Finally, despite all I've said, you don't want to be so timid and careful at your bachelor party, as to end up doing something that everybody (meaning parents, grandparents, the bridal party, and your minister) agrees is "good clean fun." Under those circumstances, you might just as well ride the pine—I don't need to tell you that you're not going to have any fun at all. The concept of "good clean fun" is not only an oxymoron, but fits neatly into those all-night drug-free, alcohol-free community New Year's Eve and post-prom bashes that well-intentioned parents and teachers throw for "the teenagers." Lots of fun games. Lots of fun music. Lots of soda pop and pretzels and pizza. Lots of smiling adults saying groovy things and patting themselves on the back for being hip enough to protect their kids from harm…and lots of nothing to talk about afterward. This is why I am *not* going to offer up a list of politically correct suggestions for a safe and happy bachelor party. As soon as you'd take me up on one, you put yourself in a position of being a good little boy—and this is no time to be a little boy. You have to be a man to be married, not someone's good little *guy*.

The bachelor party is indeed your last fling—and it is indeed *your* fling. So you define the terms. You decide up front what you want to do and where you want to do it. And it is up to you to make sure you don't step over the line in any of them. There are limits to the most far-flung of flings.

Chapter 10

Shooting for the (Honey) Moon

*A*hhhhhhhhhh...the honeymoon. The sweet dessert.

Among other important functions, the honeymoon is designed to allow newlyweds to get to know each other again—in every way—without the intrusion of family, friends, jobs, and, above all, the wedding planning that has been keeping them apart for months. It is not so much the slam dunk that ends the championship game or the big gaudy party that celebrates the ring as it is the sum of the sweet private moments in the days that follow where the couple tastes and savors their love. It is the ambrosia-like cake after the wedding cake has been cut.

Like pretty much everything else associated with engagements and weddings, the honeymoon has so much romantic mystique and myth associated with it that many couples truly believe that they will be hopping on a plane or a boat and landing in a modern-day all-inclusive version of the Garden of Eden...perfect love, perfect sex, perfect food, perfect weather....

As you might well imagine, however, such high expectations predictably lead to the kind of disappointment and resentment that can not only ruin a perfectly wonderful wedding trip, but can follow the couple out of the garden like a dark cloud over their first days and weeks and months of married life.

Julie Isaacson, who has been a travel consultant for the entertainment industry for more than 20 years, says that the key to a successful honeymoon is "to be honest about expectations...and be realistic."

Part of being realistic while still maintaining the romance, she says, is the first and maybe the most important rule of honeymoon travel: "Choose a place together that you both have an interest in." That is, don't be a saint and agree to go to a Caribbean resort just because your fiance loves to snorkel. If you don't like sun and sand, and snorkeling seems as interesting as watching water boil, the honeymoon is going to be a bust, no matter how hard you try. Conversely, if your beloved doesn't love golf nearly as much as you do, don't insist on a golf resort—and make sure you don't fall prey to her offer to go to that golf resort "if that will make you happy." Guaranteed: Your dream of playing 36 holes a few strokes above par, having a beer, and then coming back to the hotel suite where you are met by your almost naked sweetheart who has been spending the last six hours preparing herself for the greatest sex of your life is just that—a dream. It's not going to happen. The reality is that while you're playing golf (and let's be honest, probably 18 or more strokes above par) your sweetheart is lying around at the pool all by herself getting angrier and angrier at you and herself for (1) agreeing to be so self-effacing that she gave up her own honeymoon happiness for you and (2) that you would not only allow her to do that but that you would actually go out and play golf anyway—and worse still, enjoy it.

Nevertheless, Isaacson adds with a twinkle in her eye, "There's a reason why so many newlyweds go to the tropics: they really do have that sultry feel."

Geri Bain, travel editor at *Modern Bride* magazine and author of *Modern Bride Honeymoons and Weddings Away* (John Wiley and Sons, 1995), writes, "Unless you plan your honeymoon together, one of you isn't going to be very happy. And by working together, neither of you will be at fault when something doesn't go exactly as planned—which seems to happen at some point in every trip—and you can laugh it off together."

Isaacson suggests sitting down soon after you've been engaged and having a heart-to-heart about your dreams and desires for a honeymoon. In fact, don't put honeymoon planning off too long thinking that you need to take care of the wedding arrangements before you turn to anything else. Travel planning—for a honeymoon or just a vacation—takes time and energy and shouldn't be done at the last second or you're not going to get what you want.

Honeymoon Style

"The first thing you'll want to discuss," Julie Isaacson explains, "is your honeymoon style. That is, when you close your eyes, where do you see yourself?" Think:

Warm weather? Snow?

Mountains? Beach?

Sightseeing? Relaxation?

Sports? Shopping?

Fancy? Laid back?

Parties and Socializing? Private and more private?

Close? Far?

United States? Foreign country?

Cruise? Resort? Travel?

You and your fiance should sit down, make a fantasy list of what you'd like to experience on the honeymoon, and then see where the lists coincide. That, in and of itself, should be fun. It's also important to make another list of things that you definitely don't want to do on your honeymoon. And while you're making that list, be sure to consider things such as fear of flying, hatred of shopping, and language barriers.

Isaacson's associate at the Protravel, Inc., Los Angelos office, Tricia Townsend, recommends that couples not limit themselves to the typical 10 or 11 most popular honeymoon destinations (Florida, Hawaii, Mexico, Jamaica, U.S. Virgin Islands, Bahamas, California, Pennsylvania, Antigua, Barbados, Puerto Rico). She says that there are superb vacation locales a little further off the beaten path that will be a little more unique and maybe even a little more exotic—places such as Morocco, Central America, or Rio de Janero. "Just because a place isn't known for accommodating honeymooners, it doesn't mean that it isn't wonderful."

Isaacson agrees with her associate to a degree, especially for older newlyweds, but warns couples about overlooking "absolutely gorgeous, romantic places just because they made somebody's top 10 list that year. They made the top 10 lists because they know how to do honeymoons very well."

Wherever the couple chooses to go, however, Isaacson recommends keeping it as simple as possible. "The important thing is that both people need to feel safe. And part of feeling safe is feeling comfortable with where you're going."

When to Go

The typical couple goes on the typical honeymoon the day (or two days) after they are married. And like most conventions, there's good reason for that as well. Your wedding will be wonderful and memorable, but it will also be a brain-drain and energy-drain of the highest caliber—and the honeymoon will not only be a reward for all the work you did and all the emotional energy you expended, but it will prove to be a fantastic way for the two of you to be quietly alone before life, jobs, colds, car problems, children, etc., conspire to take you away from each other. You'll not only deserve it, you'll need it!

Those issues are also good reasons to put the big honeymoon off for a while and just do a quick weekend trip to some romantic destination nearby. In fact, Isaacson says that many couples report that they're simply too fatigued after all the wedding planning and excitement to fully relax and enjoy themselves. "As you can imagine, it's all pretty much a whirlwind from bachelor parties to rehearsal dinners to the ceremony and then the reception...and you might need a little distance before hopping on a plane or a boat. Or sometimes you just can't get away from work long enough to really do it right."

That said, there's the potential for a slight drawback in putting off the honeymoon for a "better time"—and Isaacson learned that firsthand. After her second marriage, she and her new husband decided to celebrate their betrothal with a quick trip, planning a much more extensive—and expensive—honeymoon a few months later to Antigua "when we'd have the time, energy, and money to really enjoy ourselves." So, right after the ceremony they got a very fancy room at the Trump Plaza in New York City and then took off for a few relaxing, romantic days and nights in the Florida Keys. "The Keys were spectacular and, of course, several months later Antigua was really wonderful. But we found out something very interesting: We now think of our honeymoon as the night at Trump and the days in the Keys because that really was our honeymoon. And Antigua turned out to be a great vacation, but it doesn't have that special place reserved in our memories for our marriage."

Something to think about...

To Travel Package or Not to Travel Package

Travel packages, as offered by airlines, credit card companies, and hotel chains, often look like great deals. They not only take care of the major arrangements (travel and accommodations), but all the annoying particulars, such as transfers, gratuities, and car rentals as well. Plus, they often throw in a few goodies, such as a complimentary meal or greens fees or snorkeling equipment. And, best of all, they look like they are saving you hundreds, if not thousands, of dollars.

Sounds very good, right? Right, except that by the time anyone is ready to get married he or she has also been through enough disappointment in life to know that things are not always what they seem. First of all, Isaacson reminds travelers that, despite appearances, "there are no huge savings to be found in packages." As with everything else in life, you get what you pay for. With that in mind, her number-one rule on travel packages is that they "must be offered by top-of-the-line products and vendors"—and that means the prices will be higher.

First, find out what they are really promising in the packages. What kind of room are you getting...a view of the beach or the pool or the laundry facility? How many square feet is the room? Julie says don't be afraid to ask, and adds, "If the package or packager says, 'Run of the House,' *run away!*" Run of the House means that they can stick you in a converted broom closet. "If you go with a package, make sure it's top of the line."

So, how do you find out who and what is top of the line? She says check out what they are offering in the package: "Read Fodors or Frommers. They are right on the money in terms of letting you know exactly what you're going to find once you arrive at your destination. Lonely Planet is also good."

She adds that magazine articles are not always 100-percent reliable, simply because the "writers may have been comped," that is, had the trip paid for by the hotel or packaging company and, short of an absolute disaster, have been inclined to treat the venue more gently than if he or she had no relationship with the company. "An effective way to measure the reliability of any of the magazines or the travel guides is to check their reports on the places you've already visited. You know exactly what you got for your money—and you know what you like. See if their impressions jibe with yours."

Cruises and All-Inclusives

If you just want to take all the pressure off and hang back and really do nothing but enjoy your honeymoon and your honey, you can't do much better than a cruise or an all-inclusive resort. Both are especially good for younger couples and folks with limited budgets because practically all your spending is done at the front end of the trip. All the financial stress and tension of pay-as-you-go, which can color each progressive day darker and darker as you watch your wallet grow thinner and thinner, is essentially eliminated.

That's exactly what happened when Patti and I went on our honeymoon 34 years ago. We left for Wales (where my brother and his wife, Florence, were living at the time) with a wad of cash and traveler's checks in our knapsacks. Wales wasn't bad, financially speaking, but we blew practically the whole amount in London and by the time we hopped the Straits and took a train to romantic Paris, we had almost nothing left but rent for a formerly charming room on the Left Bank—no great French food, no side trips to Versailles, no cab fare, not even tokens for the underground. We walked everywhere in the great city eating bread and cheese and drinking cheap wine like it was water. Not bad, I must admit—I loved every moment of it—but in retrospect it's clear the honeymoon would not have been ruined by some exquisite French food, a trip to Versailles, some clubbing, or even a charming if snarling cab driver to take us from one end of the beautiful city to the other.

At all-inclusives and cruises you can eat, sleep, and drink as much as you want—there are very few decisions to be made other than when to go to eat and what kind of food you want to stuff yourselves with.

Cruises offer additional benefits:

1. You can see many beautiful destinations in one shot.
2. Your entertainment, activities, meals, and bed are never more than a few steps away.
3. No packing and unpacking.

4. Food is abundant.
5. Being out on the ocean in a big cruise liner is a very romantic way to spend a week.

Of course, there are some downsides and issues to consider before signing on for a cruise. If you're the least bit claustrophobic or footloose, keep in mind that you will not only be stuck on board for most of the trip, but your cabin is going to be a lot smaller than most hotel rooms. Also, you will be constantly dealing with (and eating with) and lounging with the same group people for the entire trip. Be prepared to be social—or at least comfortably anti-social.

Another factor to consider about cruises, especially the big cruise liners, is that, by and large, they are patronized by senior citizens. Although younger travelers are certainly climbing on board in much greater numbers these days, cruise liners still appeal primarily to the older crowd.

As with everything else to do with honeymoons, though, don't dismiss them out of hand just because you might run into some old folks. My son, Cael, and his wife took a honeymoon cruise through the Caribbean and had the most wonderful time of their lives—and mingled with lots of younger travelers along the way. And then there's this from Julie Isaacson: "One of my newlywed clients went on a big boat to Alaska with, as it turned out, an older crowd. After their initial shock and horror, however, they loved it—the whole thing! They found that they were free to be by themselves most of the time; and they loved being treated like 'the grandkids' when they wanted to be around others. It was perfect for them."

Many of the same issues apply to all-inclusives, although the age thing is not one of them. However, you will be "stuck" in one place and you will be dealing with the same people pretty much the whole time you're there. Isaacson advises asking about food options at all-inclusives, saying that "you will need a minimum of two or three dining choices" or the experience is going to get a little dull in just a couple of days. Also, you want to find out when the dining rooms are open. "If they don't give you enough time to eat—or snack—on your own schedule, you're either hungry or spending money that you hadn't planned on spending."

Costs

The next thing to consider while planning your honeymoon is money. According to the *Modern Bride* Honeymoon Market Report, the average honeymoon lasts nine days and costs approximately $3,500.

First, don't drop your jaw or roll your eyes. You and your honeymoon are not average in any way—this is a very special time in what you hope will be the only marriage you ever know, so do it the way that feels best to you. You can take a perfectly wonderful trip on the cheap almost anywhere in the world. Conversely, you can also go luxury first class wherever you go—home or abroad. Whatever the case, go where you can afford to go. The last thing you want to be thinking about on your honeymoon is going broke.

Working With a Travel Consultant

Of course, any travel consultant with a pulse is going to suggest that you work with a trip planner for your honeymoon arrangements. That said, unless one of you has a lot of free time to research the possibilities and (as often as not) make a decision based on wishful thinking, you are best off working directly with a travel consultant. Townsend says, "It takes a lot of pressure off the couple" at a time when all they know is mounting pressure from friends, family, and wedding planners, all of whom want decisions made yesterday. She also points out that travel agents often have firsthand knowledge of the places to which honeymooners are going. If they don't have the knowledge, they certainly have reliable reports from other customers. You don't want to leave your honeymoon arrangements to chance (unless you're into that sort of thing).

Ultimately, experienced travel planners have all the necessary background to deal with any and all logistical troubles as they arise on any vacation. And all it takes is a call to get them acting on your behalf if plane reservations get screwed up, the hotel overbooks, you lose your wallet, or a hurricane is forecast in three days, or the many other eventualities that probably won't happen. But in case they do, you need to be prepared.

The question then is: how do you go about finding a reputable *and* knowledgeable travel consultant?

First, ask reliable, knowledgeable, and well-traveled friends and relatives about their travel experiences. For example, my old friend Stacy Schenker, who vacations often and maintains an extensive cross-indexed filing system of travel-related items that the American Board of Travel Agents would admire, is a terrific source of information. In contrast, another old friend, who shall remain nameless and hasn't been any place other than Disneyland for the past couple of decades, would not be such a great source for reliable information. Keep in mind, though, that both of them would be more than happy and willing to advise me on destination options.

Julie Isaacson suggests also consulting the annual issue *of Travel and Leisure* magazine, which lists the 125 best "leisure agents" in the country. They know. It doesn't matter if none of the 125 are in your area. The Internet and phone are perfect for making the contact—and snail mail and e-mail certainly are effective substitutes for sitting across a cluttered desk while glancing through piles of glossy brochures while an agent types furiously at a computer terminal.

Money, Travelers Checks, Credit Cards, Gold Bullion, Wampum

This one's simple: take travelers checks. I know, you hate travelers checks. I hate them myself. I don't know what it's all about, but most men, it seems, detest travelers checks. This may be because we don't really see why you have to use money that's a substitute for money. Nevertheless, I have this on very good word from more than a dozen travel consultants: take travelers checks…but that doesn't mean leaving all your cash and credit cards behind.

Travelers checks are recommended across the board by travel professionals not only because almost every place takes them, but because they are not susceptible to daily exchange rate swings, they are 100-percent protected, and when they are lost or stolen, they can be replaced within 24 hours.

The one thing you must take care of with regard to travelers checks is to make sure that you leave a record of the checks you have and the ones you've used. Keep one record with you in a safe place—not in your wallet or your suitcase or your hotel room—so that if something happens, you can locate the numbers and report the loss right away. As a backup, leave a copy of the record with a reliable person at home.

As vital as it is to rely on travelers checks, it is also recommended that you always have some local currency in your pocket for cab rides, tips, impulse buying, haggling with street vendors, cups of coffee, or vending machines.

Then there are credit cards (my favorite mode of travel): I don't need to remind you of the dangers of credit cards when you're having a good time. Plus, they are not so quickly replaced in the event they're lost or stolen. And, beyond that, you will find that exchange rates are variable and quite high. However, credit cards certainly make an excellent emergency backup when you've lost or spent all your travelers checks and cash. The advice from here is to bring a few credit cards, but don't use them unless it's an emergency.

How to Pack for Your Honeymoon

How much is enough? How much is too much? Although I know you are already anticipating—and hoping for—advice along the lines of "less is more," Isaacson and a couple of other travel professionals I interviewed said that you should pack as much as you want—Especially women. "Bring your favorite things...within reason," she says (without quantifying what reason means). "A little too much is better than not enough. You don't want to find yourself getting all dressed up and not having the right shoes to wear. The rule is to bring enough so that you don't have to buy anything while on vacation."

Jewelry

The one thing that you definitely don't want to pack, however, is valuable jewelry. Leave the bling bling safe at home home. "Bring fakes if you must," Isaacson says, "but never travel with expensive jewels. It's too dangerous and too disheartening if anything gets lost or stolen. It can ruin the honeymoon altogether."

Suitcases

It is generally agreed that suitcases should be light and have wheels. It is also understood that it's as important to prepare your carry-on bags as it is to efficiently pack the bigger bag(s). In the event that your bags get lost or routed to St. Louis (which happens more often than we care to acknowledge), the carry-on is literally your lifeline to the next day's survival.

Carry-ons Are Critical

With that in mind, ALL prescriptions, toiletries, identifications and money, a change of underwear, etc., should be safely stowed in the carry-ons or in your own pockets. Trish, tells a funny and outrageous yet cautionary tale about a famous entertainment-world couple whose bags were misplaced en route to a very out-of-the-way honeymoon paradise. Were they annoyed? Of course. Were they inconvenienced? Yes. Was it the end of the world? No, of course, not—they had enough cash and cache to take care of anything and everything they needed—that is, until she realized later that evening that she didn't have her birth control of choice. Now that may not be a disaster for you or me—or 99 percent of other travelers—we would simply figure out alternative arrangements to the singular dream of honeymoon bliss. But Townsens's famous couple had options and expectations of which most of us wouldn't even dream: so they chartered a plane to fly back to Los Angelos where someone would refill the prescription and send it back before midnight!

So, unless that doesn't sound utterly and completely outrageous to you, make sure you pack what really needs packing in your carry-on. And along with all the absolute necessities of life for one day, make sure both of you take along a list of the following items:

1. Serial numbers of travelers checks.
2. Emergency numbers (family, medical, travel agent, U.S. consulate, hotel).
3. Packing list.
4. Prescriptions.
5. Health insurance information.

Insurance

This piece is also very simple. Every travel consultant with whom I spoke made the same recommendation: you definitely need to buy trip cancellation insurance—no ifs, ands, or buts. And it is especially important for packages and cruises, which typically have very strict cancellation policies.

FYI: Travel insurance isn't like the bogus extended warranties for televisions and DVDs and cell phones that Circuit City and Best Buy try to sell you every time you make a purchase. This is the real deal.

You're spending a lot of money up front when planning a trip that will probably not take place for several months and—please forgive my raining on your wedding parade—you simply do not know what's going to happen to your life in the interim. No one does. Without getting too maudlin, you need to consider how family problems, sickness, death, broken engagements, broken legs, nasty bosses, bad weather, pink slips, and worthless financial portfolios can interfere with the best laid plans of brides and grooms.

So don't tempt fate. I know you feel very special, but in the broader sense, none of us are special enough to be protected from the vagaries of life, even in the golden period before we get married. And don't be cheap. For a very reasonable fee, cancellation insurance can save you a bundle.

Julie Isaacson advises buying the insurance through an outside insurance carrier—that is, do *not* buy a policy through the vacation vendor. "If, God forbid, the vendor goes bankrupt—and it does happen—then you're out of luck." Go to a reputable insurance carrier.

Troubleshooting

We keep hearing the same thing: everything changed after September 11, 2001. Well, in general that may or may not be true, but it is definitely true with regard to efficient and happy travel. It comes down to this: Failure to comply with some pretty simple guidelines (whether you agree with them or not) may easily result in being detained long enough to miss your flight or boat—or worse, being subjected to a search of body cavities. You must:

1. Check with the state department (*www.travel.state.gov*) for travel advisories, in the days and weeks before you leave for your honeymoon, if you're leaving the country. Conditions overseas change daily. Be sure you know what you're headed into.
2. Get to the airport at least two hours ahead of the departure time—and three if you're traveling overseas. No more doing the "OJ Dash" around fellow travelers and over suitcases. Be there early; the plane waits for no one, not even honeymooners. Once you're there, wait patiently while the labor-intensive process of checking in takes place. Be prepared to remove your shoes, jewelry, belts,

cell phones, and anything else that will trip a metal detector. In fact, you may want to plan you travel outfit accordingly. If you have a metal plate in your body, or wear a pacemaker, or—as in the case of a friend of mine who was shot by her husband (Note: Good husbands don't ever shoot their wives)—doctors were unable to remove a bullet from your body, carry a note from your doctor explaining the metal in your body. One more note: You might find, as Patti and I did on our last flight out of LaGuardia Airport in New York that the e-ticket checking in process and the subsequent security check went smoothly and quickly, leaving us with more than an hour before we would be able to board the flight. You can't plan on that, however, and it does no good to get annoyed at anyone or anything. It is what it is—plan ahead to grab a bite to eat or read a magazine.

3. Be sure that neither of you packs anything with a sharp or pointy edge. That includes seemingly harmless objects such as penknives, nail clippers, nail files, etc. (Also, just for the record, in case someone out there thinks the inspectors are just looking for the small things, don't try to bring weapons or any illicit drugs on the plane—then the search of body cavities is the least of your worries.)

4. Don't pack cameras loaded with film in the bags that you check, the scanning devices may ruin the pictures.

5. Don't make any jokes whatsoever about hijacking, terrorists, weapons, or the like. In fact, don't even utter those words. Whether it is reasonable or not, people's ears and fears are highly sensitized these days to any hint toward a terror attack—and all it would take to find yourself naked and shackled in a windowless room at the airport is for someone to overhear you saying something about hijacking.

6. If at all possible, avoid buying one-way tickets. Julie Isaacson advises that one-way tickets are much more likely to invite the scrutiny of law enforcement officials than round trippers. Just keep that in mind when considering time arrangements.

Fear of Flying

Fear of flying—or anxiety related to travel away from home of any kind—is far more common than you may think. The critical factor in making travel less stressful, says psychologist Marj Steinfeld, whom we heard from previously, is "Don't fight it, work with it. Resisting your fears is often not only futile, but exacerbates them in the process."

If getting on a plane creates overwhelming anxiety, it is not only going to ruin the trip en route to your dream vacation, it's probably going to cast a dark cloud on the entire honeymoon as you anticipate moving closer and closer to the horrid trip home. If you can get there by train, boat, car, whatever, just acknowledge the anxiety and do it. If there's no way to get to where you want to go except by plane, go someplace else. It's not worth the misery.

That said, if your anxiety about planes or travel in general is more moderate, that is, not severe enough to stop you, you can modulate it in a number of ways.

1. **Meditation/visualization.** As a health educator, I have researched and utilized many effective meditation and visualization techniques over the years. And without trying to sound too coy, they do work very well for the people for whom they work. I know that sounds like a nonanswer, but it's true about most therapies—you have to try it out to see if it works for you. It is difficult to learn meditation or visualization on your own, so I'd recommend joining a local group (you can find one most anywhere). Check them out. If joining a group is not realistic, I'd recommend Chakti Gawain's *Creative Visualization* (New World Library, 2002) as a terrific way to learn simple techniques for detaching yourself from paralyzing thoughts and anxieties. A good meditation handbook, according to Dahli Bartz-Cabe, a spiritual guide from Walden, New York, is *Wherever You Go, There You Are* (Hyperion, 1995) by Jon Kabat-Zinn.

2. **Natural remedies for anxiety.** Julie Isaacson reports that many of her clients take care of pre-flight nervousness with old-time remedies such as a glass of warm milk or

new age vitamin therapies such as taking melatonin or magnesium. Others, of course, take one good shot (never any more) of whiskey to bolster their courage. Here again, check these options out long before you go on the trip if anxiety plagues you. You don't want to be running field trials of anxiety suppressors while sitting in a pool of sweat on the airplane. Trish says that many clients report that Valium or Ambien works very well for travel anxiety. My son-in-law Jeffrey, who hates to fly, says that his honeymoon to Sicily was saved by Atavin. He recently wrote, "...it's not the strongest drug, but it's a sweetheart—I recently talked down the nut job next to me on my way back from Seattle and he was on something much stronger."

Dr. Marj concurs but cautions that you must consult with your doctor or therapist before dosing yourself. And here again, you should know, before you get on the plane, whether the remedy works for you.

Legal Problems Away from Home

As Isaacson says, "You must be really stupid to travel with illegal drugs or weapons or contraband of any sort when you go on a trip." Just don't do it—whatever it is. All of us know basically what is legal or not—and keep in mind that whatever legal troubles you can get yourself into in the United States might seem mild compared to the horrible predicament you'll find yourselves in another country. You don't want to end up on the evening news.

That said, if for any reason you find yourself in a legal mess while out of the country, the first two calls to make are (1) to the United States consulate and (2) to some reliable, un-hysterical somebody at home who will be willing and able to monitor your situation and advocate for you.

Sickness

Not much to do if you feel really sick on your honeymoon. Treat yourself just as you would at home. And don't push yourself to be the "good spouse" and get yourself really sick. However, if the illness or injury moves beyond the take-aspirin-and-push-fluids stage, the hotel concierge or tour operator will be able to recommend local doctors or hospitals. Think ahead and consult your physician about common maladies such as diarrhea, motion sickness, or flu. And if you are really, really sick—and really don't want to stay in a hospital where you are—Isaacson says that Medjet is a great company for quick departures.

Accommodating Your Accommodations Problems

If you arrive at your hotel room and are greeted by a marching band of cockroaches, do what you can on your own with the hotel/tour manager or supervisor to remedy the situation. Be assertive. However, if you get no satisfaction, call the travel agent who arranged the trip. Isaacson says you can call a travel agent 24/7 and she/he will not only advocate for you, but should know who to contact and what to say to make that advocacy more than just talk.

Finally, If the Whole Thing Is a Bust

What happens if the trip of your most romantic dreams turns out to be a chapter out of your worst nightmare?

Townsend: If the accommodations or the tour are not salvageable, a good travel agent can reroute you to a place that is more to your liking.

Isaacson: If everything is miserable, I'd just go home and spend all the money (that you're going to get back) on things that are fun. You'll laugh about it as soon as the sting of the disappointment is past.

Dr. Steinfeld: Don't wait to laugh about it in a few years. Find the humor in the situation as it is and make the best of it. After all, you're together and you are in love. Love—and a good sense of humor—conquers all. (Check Chapter 15.)

Part III
June Madness

Chapter 11

A Gentle Reminder:
Something in the Way She Moves

*Y*ou know, sometimes in the midst of all those momentous decisions about things such as cake color, floral arrangements, high level contentious negotiations about the invitation list, and the growing realization of the serious responsibilities that go along with engagements, weddings, and marriage, we sometimes lose sight of why we're making all those lists and decisions and why we are inviting all those new responsibilities into our lives: Because you love her with all your heart and can't imagine spending another day of your life without her.

It is a good thing to remind yourself of that singularly romantic fact from time to time because all that thinking and planning makes for a lot of upset stomachs, hot heads, and cold feet. Causing extreme confusion—in the form of cold stomachs, upset heads, and hot feet—is the undeniable fact that at the very core of this whole experience is a love that nobody understands and nobody is able to control.

Although this book is full of advice on how to prepare for what is arguably the most important day of your life and all the days thereafter, the best advice I can offer you at this point is" don't try to understand why it's all so important. Just accept that it is *important* for no other reason than you love her, and then move ahead.

Each August I spend hours a day on the beach on Hatteras Island, North Carolina, just watching the parade of couples walking hand in hand along the shoreline. Fat ones. Skinny ones. Old ones. Young ones. Some are as beautiful as the blue Carolina sky, and some, frankly, are as butt ugly as their butts, which you have to turn away from as soon as your eyes fall on them. Sometimes it all gets mixed up and you see fat and skinny ones together holding hands, or young and old with their fingers entwined—or any combination that doesn't seem to go together in the natural order of the universe.

Yet every summer I have the same revelation: there is someone for everyone in this world. And it seems as if we are hotwired at birth to grow up and find that someone to love and share our days (and our genetic material).

Just consider your own circumstances. Isn't it amazing that she, among all the others, is the one with whom you found your destiny to love? All those women out there on the beach and you fell in love with the one you (I dare say, almost predictably) would never have chosen for yourself in the thinking part of your brain if the thinking part of your brain had anything to do with the decision. It's a conundrum of overwhelming proportions.

Maybe you just saw her across a room and fell head-over-heels in love with her. Perhaps you've seen her every day for years, but one morning as she lifted a cup of coffee to her lips, you suddenly found yourself madly, desperately, passionately in love with her. Or maybe you knew her and loved her in 8th grade. The truth is that it doesn't matter whether it was love at first sight or love as an oversight, the sudden metamorphosis is the most amazing part of the whole thing. Suddenly her scent makes you tingle. Her skin tantalizes you. Her smile calls you. She is, in the space of a single breath, the most beautiful creature with the most wonderful eyes you have ever seen. It's all quite miraculous—and marvelous—and utterly mysterious.

This is why you shouldn't try too hard to understand what it's all about. Don't attempt to quantify or qualify your love. That is, don't think you love her because she likes the Green Bay Packers and so do you, or that you appreciate the same books or movies, or that she's your body type, or that she's blond or has high cheekbones, or that she's kind to dogs and old men. All of that is very nice (or not nice), but it has absolutely nothing to do with why you fell in love with her and not someone else.

Above all, don't try to control it. Control your anxiety, your temper, your gambling, your drinking, eating, and smoking. Control your pocketbook, as the evil Iago says, control your best man, if that's possible. Control as many of the nuts and bolts of life that you can in order to hold the ship together, but don't try to control the way that you love—or the person that you love.

Move your way into your beloved's future with a willingness to experience the everything that's coming your way. As Siddhartha tells his friend Govinda in what I suspect is the most brilliant passage in all of literature—*Siddhartha* by Herman Hesse (Bantam, 1981)—"Everything is necessary, everything needs only my agreement, my assent, my loving understanding; then all is well with me and nothing can harm me." Move along hand in hand. There is no way to escape either the joy or the sorrow of life. (If you've never read this book, go get yourself a copy. It's like an insurance policy against feeling overwhelmed by daily life.)

So, let me tell you about my mysterious babe:

Patricia Charlee Henderson is a patrician, a blue blood, raised in the Garden District of New Orleans, groomed at Miss Edith Akins Little School and later refined at the Louise S. McGhee School on Prytannia Street. She actually understands *noblesse oblige*.

I'm a New York Jew, spawned out of the generational pickle juice of Brooklyn, kidnapped to Flushing, and raised in a suburban development of quarter acre ranchers bulldozed out of a Long Island potato field. I went to public school in a cranky yellow bus; itched my way through Wheatley High in an ugly succession of mohair sweaters, khaki pants, and white socks; and played three sports without ever learning grace under pressure. I did learn about obligations, however, by way of the adolescent charms of a girl named Judy Goldstein.

Patricia Charlee Henderson and I met purely by accident in September 1964 as newly arrived freshmen at the University of Wisconsin. Despite the red Wisconsin sweatshirt and the red plaid slacks, I thought she was beautiful: gorgeous face, long brown hair, the hollow in the sway of her back that instantly created a yearning in the hollow of my throat. I have no idea what she thought about me that afternoon, but it wasn't until more than three years later—a long generally uninteresting story during which time she dated (off and on) my roommate—we had our first date on December 10, 1967.

I know the exact date because I had two tickets to see the great Otis Redding in Madison. And that was the fateful night, on the way to the performance, that Mr. Redding's plane crashed into the frozen waters of Lake Monona. An inauspicious beginning to the relationship—certainly—but we were married the following August.

Thirty-five years later, I still don't understand. We have nothing of the usual things in common. Nothing. Sports, plays, crafts, music, antiquing...nothing. (I later found out that she didn't even like the great Otis Redding.) I am drawn to her daily in vast unspeakable ways, a vague sense of biological inevitability when we pass in the hall or even in separate cars; or later, when I inhale her scent, or feel her breath in my ear.

I like her. I like who she is. Don't ask me why. We somehow share the same vision of life. Again, don't ask me why. Beyond that it's pure mystery.

In truth, if you had asked me to describe my ideal partner 35 years ago, it could have been almost anyone but Patti Henderson. (I might easily have said something like "She is absolutely beautiful, but she's not my style.") Yet since the moment I first haltingly placed my lips on hers, it has been she with whom I have always had to be. No one else. No one else. I can't repeat that too many times.

I have tried in vain to explain to my friends and even some nosy strangers about the desire and the ambivalence and the roots of a relationship that not only connects us, but has somehow inspired us to bring seven children into this universe. As Stella says to Blanche in *A Streetcar Named Desire*, "There are things that happen between a man and a woman in the dark...." Things. As Katherine Mansfield wrote in Jon Winokur's *Zen to Go* (Plume, 1991), "Wind moving through grass so that grass quivers. This moves me with an emotion that I don't even understand."

And, mostly, things in the dark, though I don't only mean things in the sack. I promise there's much more than that. Much more. Though it's hard to be more specific. Patti and I are together all this time *and* have seven kids because of who we are and who we are to each other. As far as I can see, there is no more acceptable explanation for our choices than there is about why some people like their oysters from the Chesapeake and others from the Rockies.

And to give this fishy stew a really bizarre flavor, let me add this: While Patti always wanted a large family—it was from earliest consciousness her sense of connection to the earth—I know myself well enough to realize that had I married someone else, I probably wouldn't have had so many children. It's even possible that I would actually have married someone who didn't want kids and would be now writing a reflection on our matched pair of Harley Sportsters.

But of course I didn't.

Nevertheless, you know what I'm talking about. These mysteries and things that happen in the dark are why you're getting married.

Now let me tell you a more contemporary story of crazy love.

There probably aren't two more unlikely marriage partners than my daughter Clover and her husband Jeffrey—unless, of course, you consider Patti and me or _____ (fill in your own candidates). Nevertheless, here's a more contemporary portrait of local bliss:

At 26 years old, Jeffrey is a meticulous, ambitious, assertively political, Yankees fan, homebody, and law student who would rather be anywhere than on an airplane or at a big boisterous party. Just beyond the law degree, nearly in his back pocket, Jeffrey dreams of being president of the United States and wants to write a massive tome titled *The World According to Jeffrey*.

Clover is...well, Clover. She's anything but meticulous (years ago, the family ran out of towels and we found 23 on her bedroom floor); and, although she dreams of saving the world one person at a time with that MSW degree just over the horizon, ambition is not quite the word to describe her, unless you're thinking beach; and if she followed any baseball team it would be the Mets. And, let's be clear: Clover loves a big party and considers intercontinental travel as essential as oxygen.

They simply could not be more different. Yet last May, Clover Lewis and Jeffrey Trapani committed the most admirable and audacious act I think anyone ever does in life: they pledged themselves to each other, body and soul, heart and mind, reality and dreams, for the rest of their lives.

Let's go back to their beginning, which is 8th grade at the New Paltz Middle School: Jeffrey is nearing 98 pounds, the scrawniest member of the wrestling team, and a heartsick boy who spends hours writing "Crimson and Clover" literally thousands of times "over and over" in his notebook. (These are the lyrics to a song by Tommy James and the Shondells, for those of you who are lost.) His room at home is clean and neat. His notebooks are neat and orderly. He wears crisp khakis and pressed button-down shirts. And for reasons no one really understands, he loves Clover Lewis with all his heart.

Now take a look at Clover in 1991, who is already 98 pounds, a gymnast, all elbows and knees with an easygoing manner and a lilting smile full of metal. Her room at home (remember the 23 towels?) is a freaking mess. Her notebooks look something like the junk mail recycling dumpster. She often shows up at school in outfits that bear a remarkable resemblance to pajamas. And for reasons no one really understands, she loves Jeffrey Trapani with all her middle-school heart.

Fast forward through four years at New Paltz High School: After more break-ups than my cell phone on a drive over the mountain, Clover and Jeffrey are still together and still in love and, somewhat ironically, both going off to college in North Carolina. But he is going to Wake Forest and she is going to UNC—and the only thing more onerous for either of them would be if the other went to Duke. (That actually might have been the deal breaker.)

Fast forward four years again: After surviving several more spats and splits and splats—and a break-up the size of the Pacific Ocean (Clover spent the year in Australia)—Clover and Jeffrey are still together in Raleigh, North Carolina—and still madly in love.

Now fast forward four years *one more time*: The 8th grade couple who most assuredly would have been voted most likely not to get married if the principal had allowed such a category, were hitched by the stream in our backyard.

A father wishes many things for his daughter, but perhaps nothing more than that she find someone who adores her the way he does—and for no other reason than that she is to that man as utterly and inexplicably loveable as anyone could ever be in the universe.

Such is Jeffrey, the meticulous homebody with big dreams and fears of flying. For 12 years I have watched Jeffrey unabashedly love my utterly wonderful footloose daughter, even after seeing her room (and the 23 towels); after waving good-bye to her as she flew off to Spain (Zimbabwe, Zambia, Kenya, Australia, Scotland, and England); and, I trust, after realizing that she will never ever ever EVER, in a million years, be his Laura Bush or Jackie Kennedy as he entertains in the Rose Garden at the White House.

I suspect they are the incarnation of eternal love. Just like you two are.

It's likely that you opened this book with a notion of the wedding season as a time of the effortless bliss with your one and only—and I have done my best to transform that simple vision into a complex series of challenges to be met head-on before seriously thinking about kids, equity, career advancement, retirement, estate planning…I'll stop right there.

You stop there as well. But just as you cannot stop your heart from pounding in her presence, don't try to answer the unanswerable. Don't label it. Don't explain it. Ponder grace, be humbled by it. Be elevated by it. Don't give it a name, or an explanation; anything you'd come up with would make it all a farce.

And, finally, consider well these lines from Emily Dickinson, the lovelorn poet from Amherst, Massachusetts:

> 'Tis opposites—entice—
> Deformed Men—ponder Grace
> Bright fires—the Blanketless
> *The Lost—Day's face—*

If it doesn't make any sense, just turn the page. If it does, commit it to memory and recite it some cozy night to your sweetheart.

Chapter 12

Weddiquette

There is no doubt in my mind that the number-one myth about the whole engagement and wedding season is the one spoken by all mothers, mothers-in-law, wedding planners, and clergy members is: *It's all about the bride and the groom.* Indeed, as each of you moves toward your wedding day, you might sometimes even believe that the whole affair is focused on you and your bride. And frankly, it's actually quite reasonable and understandable that anybody would make that assumption. It should be just about you and your bride.

I'm sorry to say, though, it is not.

In fact, it's comparable to the same myth that plagues all professional athletes: *It's all about the game...the pure pursuit of something someone loves more than anything in the world.*

Wrong. Just as all NBA players are beholden to everyone connected with the decision to make basketball a career (owners, agents, fans, sponsors, teammates, spouses, girlfriends, groupies, opponents, journalists, and law enforcement officials), so too are engaged men beholden to a whole association of people who believe that someone else's wedding is a singularly momentous event in their lives.

Indeed, even in that pure and golden moment when you find yourself standing in front of the altar watching your beautiful bride walking down the aisle to promise to give herself to you, body and soul, for all the days of your lives, you may believe that the world around you two ceases to exist.

Nope.

If you'll just wipe the moisture from your brow and the tears from your eyes, you'll see very clearly that there is a whole arena out there cheering (and sometimes silently booing) for your happiness. You bring a lifetime of experiences and connections and baggage to the ceremony. Out in the pews (or the folding chairs...or standing on the lawn...or out the beach...or in the judge's office...or at the reception), there are more people than you might imagine who believe that they have a real stake in making your wedding day as special and joyous and memorable as possible.

Just for the record, let's count some of them:

1. Grandparents, parents and—more and more frequently—children and grandchildren, each of whom somehow believes that he or she alone is instrumental in getting you where you are at that moment.
2. Aunts, uncles, cousins, godparents, friends, business associates, etc., all of whom bring all their private wishes to your wedding, praying for everything from sex to romance to business connections to being discovered by someone from Hollywood or American Idol to simply forgetting their troubles for a few hours.
3. Caterers, wedding planners, florists, bakers, photographers, bartenders, etc., each of whom is not only trying to make your day a good one but marketing themselves shamelessly to everyone else on the invitation list.
4. Priests, rabbis, pastors, judges, Internet ministers, ship captains and the various institutions that they represent, including God Himself or Herself.
5. You and your future wife. In the sweetest of all possible ways, each of you wants even more than your own happiness for that special day, pure joy for your mate.

And finally, but probably not finally

6. All the future generations that will flow from your seed and who will one day trace their fortunes back to your special day to see whether or not you acted like a gentleman or a heel.

That's a lot of people and a lot of pressure. And because each of those people or groups have a stake in your happiness—or at least in the rewards that come with your satisfaction—you in turn have a stake in their happy memories of the day. It may not be fair—and it may not be what you want—but such is life. And, as such, there are 10 Commandments for proper wedding etiquette that, for your bride, your own well-being, and the untold fortunes of your heirs, are definitely worth heeding.

The 10 Commandments

At the Ceremony

1. **Honor Thy Father and Thy Mother** (but mostly your mother). Remember the first day of kindergarten? Remember the look on your mother's face? Make sure your hair is cut and combed, your face is neatly shaved, your shirt tucked in, your fly is closed, your shoes are shined and tied, your shirt is white, your socks are black, your nails are cut, and your underwear is clean. Don't pick your nose. Don't bite your fingernails. Stand up straight, please. Your mother has been saying these things to you your whole life. For once, don't let her down.

2. **Thou Shalt Not Do Shtick at the Ceremony.** No smirking, gesturing, high fives, fraternity handshakes, gang signs, or under-the-breath comments to your groomsmen during the wedding march or ceremony. No final bonding moments with your best man or your brother. This isn't Midnight Madness at the Dean Dome. This isn't your final gasp as a single guy (that happened at your bachelor party). Also, it is not funny or wise or forgivable to look around expectantly or wistfully when the officiator asks if there is anyone present who has reason to object to the marriage. Don't play to the crowd. Don't pretend that you lost—or dropped—the ring. It's just you two—in front of everyone you know.

3. **Thou Shalt Not Covet Thy Fraternity Brother's Date.** Your flirting days are over. Stick a fork in them. Maybe you can take the old song and dance out of mothballs once a year for the annual office Christmas party, but

that's about it. This is your wedding. No ogling. No elbows. No eye contact with your best friend when your friend Paul's date, a waitress at Hooters, sashays into the cermony. No lewd comments (even under your breath). You may not even nod your head in response to a lewd comment made by your Uncle Herman about the girl with the slit up the side of her dress. In fact, you are not allowed to compliment any other woman at the wedding on her looks, except, of course, your mother, mother-in-law, and aunts older than the age of 55. Although you are not in court, you're on the court of public scrutiny and everybody's watching and wondering why you're acting so disrespectful to the woman you love.

4. **Thou Shalt Not Have Strange Gods Before You.** Turn off your cell phone. Seriously. Please, please, please. Better still, leave it home with your beeper. This shouldn't need an explanation.

5. **Thou Shalt Not Cry.** No uncontrollable crying, weeping, bawling, or excessive ferklempting. And definitely no howling. Misting is okay. Welling up is fine, even admirable. Think about how you'd like to play the final seconds of a championship game: powerful emotions in check.

At the Reception

6. **Thou Shalt Not Be a Glutton.** Don't eat yourself sick. Don't drink yourself into a stupor. Don't puke. Don't ingest anything that blemishes your boyish good looks. Don't do eat, drink, smoke, snort anything to imperil your ability to perform your manly duties later that evening.

7. **Thou Shalt Not Be a Boor.** When everybody pings their champagne glasses, don't slip a tongue into your bride's mouth. When you're out on the dance floor showcasing your moves, don't grab your crotch. If you're white, try to stop yourself from doing the "white man's overbite." If you're not white, don't even think about doing the "white man's overbite." Later on, if you're going to remove her garter with your teeth, don't leer, and,

above all, don't do that stupid thing that some men do with their tongues that they think girls think is appealing. It is *appalling*, not appealing. There is not a woman alive who thinks it's sexy. And do I have to mention that your pants need to stay on all night? And your fly needs to be zipped?

8. **Thou Shalt Dance With Your Mother.** And her mother. And with each of the grandmothers. And don't dirty dance with any of them (even if they're willing), or anyone else. In fact, don't dirty dance with your bride. Let your buddies or fraternity brothers and her single friends take care of all the necessary and unnecessary dirty dancing for you.

9. **Thou Shalt Schmooze.** You may hate this commandment worse than you hate going to the dentist, but as the cohost and raison d'etre of the affair, you are called upon to visit every table at the reception and make pleasant happy small talk with everyone you recognize. That's right, *every* table. You must also laugh right along with all the old men and their predictable "first night" and Viagra jokes. (Please don't try to explain that you've been living together for the last two years.) You must hold the handkerchief holding hands of the widowed and maiden aunts who tell you to be good to her. You must practice smiling your most sincere smile while saying 75 or 80 times, to every one of her uncles, each of whom will not fail to tell you what a great catch you landed, "I am the luckiest guy in the world."

10. **Thou Shalt Not Kill the Holy Moment.** This is the big one. Never ever push cake in her face! Ever. Really.

    I can't repeat this too many times—it is truly a bad thing to do. I'm not sure where this strange ritual began—or why anyone thinks it's funny to humiliate the woman of your dreams—but any way you look at it, every way that you play it, there are at least 11 good reasons for not pushing cake in your beloved's face. Memorize them all:

1. It is always humiliating to the person whose face is being shoved into flour and sugar. She may laugh, but she will never think it was funny.
2. It is, when you get all the way down to the heart of the matter, an abusive thing to do, no matter who's doing it.
3. No matter who's doing it, it marks a very bad start for the marriage.
4. You'll likely stain her dress and ruin her $100 makeup job. Not to be underestimated in terms of long-term payback.
5. She will not only want to get you back for publicly humiliating her, she will. (She will...)
6. Her father, who is already half in the bag from pride, despair, bankruptcy, and the open bar, will want to kill you when he sees you abusing his baby girl. He may not kill you right then and there (or he might), but be assured that he will do everything in his power from then on in to cut your walnuts off your tree.
7. From behind your mother's frozen smile, there will be a little twinge of fury and sadness that she did not do enough to raise a son who would respect women. You do not want to do that to your good mother. (See Commandment #1.)
8. The forlorn—and drunk—guy you beat out for your lovely bride's hand in marriage, might see the cake smushed into her flaring nostrils and see it as one last opportunity to show her how much he loves her. Like Zorro he will race to the center of the room and punch your lights out.
9. Everyone in the entire wedding party will know in their hearts that you are a heel. And some day—in ways that you can't even begin to predict or understand—being a public heel will come back to haunt you. It always does.
10. I know I'm in no position to say this—and I know that it smacks of real arrogance and heresy—but I do say with all sincerity that God will some day punish you for pushing cake in your bride's beautiful face.

11. Let's be frank here. Even if you don't buy into any of these absolutely reliable warnings, here's one that might at least give you pause before you press the icing against her powdered nose: this will not be the only chance you have to push cake in your beloved's face. There will be ample opportunity after you're married for both of you to push cake in the other's face in the privacy of your own home. Trust me.

Chapter 13

Sex and the Not-So-Single Guy

*I*n a recent National Council of Psychiatrists study of 2,000 men, it was reported that males have sexual thoughts and fantasies approximately once every 18 seconds. (No, that's not a misprint. Just think about it for 18 seconds.) So, it is not overstating the case to say that sex is a major factor in practically everything men do. As such, sex is urging us on to the altar and the delights beyond and it's a pretty good bet that the gloriously famous "wedding night" has a significance that goes way beyond what it reasonably should.

(*Quick note*: With the above statistic in mind, the odds are pretty good that this is the first chapter you're glancing through en route to deciding whether you're going to buy this book—or, in the case that someone else (your mother, girlfriend, girlfriend's mother, girlfriend's friend) bought it for you, whether or not you're actually going to sit down and read it. So, notwithstanding any personal bias I may have in making a recommendation, my suggestion is to go ahead and read what lies ahead—and behind—if for no other reason than that I guarantee that this chapter alone will save you hours, days, months, and years of frustration, despair, and what I refer to as stuck-in-traffic-manual-alopecia—or tearing one's hair out. It may even bring you right onto the wide open highway of lifelong sexual pleasure in your very own spanking red Ferrari.)

First Time–Long Time *or* Long Time–Long Time

Whether you're a card carrying member of the Walt Chamberlain Society (you've been up and down the court more times than you remember) or you've been playing one-on-none or sexual air hoops on your own private court since you were 13 years old (and, in effect, saving yourself for your wedding night), there is not a heterosexual man alive who is not looking forward with great glee to watching the wedding gown fall off his bride as a tantalizing prelude to that first glorious night of sex in what promises to be a lifetime of legal pleasures.

That said, there are also very few men in the universe who are so comfortable with their sexuality that they are aren't even modestly daunted by the huge expectations (male, female, or Spice-channel) for them to perform essentially superhuman miracles in bed on that special evening. For better or worse, you will be sharing the bed on that first night with thousands of years of culture, lore, and myth about how wedding night sex is supposed to go.

So, recapping the pregame show:

1. Everybody's looking forward to that first night of wild passionate married sex.
2. Whether you like it or not, everybody shares the bed that first night with thousands of years of culture, lore, and myth about how wedding night sex is supposed to go.
3. There are probably only seven men on the North American continent who are not even a little nervous about having to perform like the sexual Olympians we think we're all supposed to be in the adoring eyes of our beloved lovers.

That's a lot of pressure. You're on the line for a one-and-one, there's one tick left on the clock, and your team is down by one point. Do the math. Blow the first one and it all lands on your shoulders for eternity. Make the first and blow the second and you avoid abject humiliation, but there's no glory in a tie; someone else is going to step up to the line. Thus, the only option is to make both free throws or the rest of your natural life will stumble from one abject humiliation to the next. You'll be the living incarnation of Charlie Brown, forever trying to kick the football as Lucy pulls it away at the last moment.

Dr. Marj Steinfeld, offers this speculation on why so many men get so (stinking) drunk on the night of their wedding: "If you get so drunk that you can't perform—which for some reason is something that men and women understand and accept as acceptable—you will not be expected to perform." And thus you're off the hook and can play more confidently before a smaller crowd the next night. She call's it "alcohol as self-medication." Others may call it throwing in the towel.

It's Not the Final Four

Of course, all that talk of Olympian orgasms and tests and performance is not only intimidating, it's very destructive to real sex between real lovers. Or so says Cynthia G. Pizzulli, Ph.D., an AASECT (American Association of Sex Educators, Counselors, and Teachers) certified sex therapist, from East Northport, New York. Dr. Pizzulli suggests that far too many couples, whether they are experienced in sexual love or not, approach the wedding night as a test to see whether their marriage is worthy. She says that there is far too much emphasis on "big bang sex," which is an "accident waiting to happen."

When the fireworks don't light up the entire sky, she says, "the larger than life expectation of wedding night sex becomes a negative fulfilling prophecy of your own sexual inadequacy." Translated: the bigger the expectations for the night, the less likely you're going to truly enjoy the first sexual experience of the rest of your married life. It's going to feel like a performance. Or worse still, it will feel like a chore. And it will set the stage for a lifetime of chores that should have been pure pleasure.

Sex Toys, Aphrodisiacs, Step-by-Step Instructions

You're not alone in hoping that this chapter is somehow going to provide you with the kind of information that will not only enable you to gain a lifetime of sexual ecstasy, but also to establish you as the best lover on the face of the Earth from the honeymoon night forward. Definitely not alone.

However, you're also not going to be surprised—just disappointed—in a few pages when Dr. Pizzulli assures you (as any other reputable sex therapist would) that there are no sex toys, no aphrodisiacs, no secret primitive techniques, and no step-by-step instructions that will allow you to fulfill all your fantasies of loving and being loved. Just consider the cover of practically every magazine aimed at men and women in their 20s and 30s (and now 40s): every single issue contains an article that identifies the five, seven, 10, or whatever number of techniques, guaranteed to bring you or your lover to the height of orgasmic ecstasy at will. Now think about this: If any of those techniques actually worked—at all—everyone would be completely satisfied and we'd never see another magazine cover promising "to drive him/her crazy in bed." Yet we do see those covers, week after week. They're not evil or bad. They just don't work. It's all smoke and mirrors and snake oil. (And, by the way, despite all the spam you're finding on your computer all day every day, there is no substance in the universe that can increase the size of your penis.)

Everything in Its Place

Now might be a good time to review Chapter 12. You've had to dance in front of the whole room with your bride, your mother, your new mother-in-law, your Aunt Sadie, your cute but obnoxious 3-year-old cousin Tiffany. You have had to visit every table in the room with a smile plastered across your weary face. You have had to endure the endless taunts and needling of every uncle on the bride's side telling you how lucky you are to be getting such a great girl (Translation: how did a piece of crap like you end up with this goddess?). And let's not forget your own uncles, elbowing you in the sore ribs and leering right in your bride's direction wondering out loud how you got so lucky (Translation: you get to sleep with her for the rest of your life).

That's a heavy load for any human being to carry into his marriage bed. As a result, far more couples than you would expect do not—or cannot (that is someone gets too drunk)—make love that night. The simple truth is that all the preparations leading up to the wedding day and night are draining—spiritually, physically, and emotionally. Please keep in mind that the wedding is exhausting when you're the one getting married.

All your guests may be running home from the reception to jump in the sack, but that's because they've been a part of a remarkably romantic event (at your cost). And let's not forget the open bar that cost someone else an arm and a leg. They've been to a great party and had a great time and are full of liquor and *l'amour*.

You, on the other hand, have had all the multiple anxieties inherent in a long season (year? several years?) of engagement possibilities, challenges and woes, all funneling into what is expected to be the most important night of anyone's life.

Taking the Edge Off

There are lots of ways to take the edge off in pressure situations, whether you're going to the line for the game winning free throw or making love to your wife for the first time: a stiff drink (just one), meditation, deep breathing, or visualization, to name a few. There's also the diversionary tactic that men have been utilizing to gain a measure of sexual control in the sack for (50? 100? 1,000?) years: make yourself think of something else (baseball or sword fights or jousting). And don't discount simply talking to your fiance honestly and openly about your anxiety. If you can do it, it will definitely help to demystify the situation. Remember, she's probably just as nervous as you are—and maybe more.

Whatever you do to calm yourself down, though, remind yourself (over and over if necessary) that despite all the hype associated with the wedding night, it's just a night—one night. And you will have a lifetime of nights ahead to make love to the one person in the world you love more than life itself.

So don't rush it. Don't push it or squash it. Simply enjoy each other's company and see where the mutual enjoyment takes you.

Going to the Bench

Another suggestion for taking the pressure off yourself—and please sit down before you read what follows because this one might shock you—is to bench yourself for the night. That's right, ride the pine. With tongue firmly planted in cheek, Dr. Pizzulli says there is nothing in the marital bylaws or the U.S. Constitution that mandates that you have to make love on your marriage night.

Just because it's expected of you, there are no hard-and-fast rules that say that couples have to heed to the old, and essentially silly, Nike phrase "Just Do It." There are not going to be any grizzly old uncles or witchy old aunts outside your door waiting to show the world the blood-stained sheets. It's just you and your bride, private and alone, as it should be.

If you do consummate your marriage on the night of your wedding—and let's be honest, almost everyone does—bully for you and her. I hope it goes beautifully. But if not, as previously mentioned, you have a lifetime of days and nights and afternoons of unimagined sexual pleasure ahead of you. And keep in mind that just by taking mandatory sex off the table for one night carries with it the distinct possibility of putting it right back there on the table where you wanted it in the first place. Such is the oxymoronic nature of sex.

In fact, in our exclusive interview, the good doctor was frank enough to share the fact that she and her husband did not make love on their wedding night. Indeed, she recounts with great humor a very funny story of her own wedding night—where she spent several frustrating hours removing a hundred hairpins from her well-coifed head while her new and very drunk husband passed out on the bed. "Making love on the first night is not a requirement for marital bliss. The days and nights afterward are the really important ones."

What Really Leads to Erotic Connections

Dr. Pizzulli, who has been counseling couples for more than 10 years on healthy and satisfying sexual relationships, says that there's far too much emphasis in this culture on technique and sexual aids and far too little on the real communication that leads to erotic connections.

"On your wedding night, it's not advisable to try anything new or exotic. This night, above all other nights, is more about sharing love and affection than pure sex." So save the gymnastic positions and sex toys and aids for later on in your relationship—or even the next night—when battery failure or dislocation of limbs might be less significant. "Just talk," she says, "about anything. You'll find that the intimacy of the night itself will take over."

Talk the Talk

Ask any woman about what turns her on and, among the hundred other things she might think of, she will tell you she wants to talk to her lover before making love. And Dr. Pizzulli adds, "That doesn't mean making conversation for five minutes before you start putting on the moves. In fact, it's the talk that occurs *before* the big night that really pays off in the bedroom."

With that in mind, Dr. Pizzulli suggests that any couple would benefit from a session—or a few sessions—before the wedding ceremony with a therapist to explore the elements of a happy and healthy emotional and sexual union. She says that it would not only help mutual understanding between bride and groom and to ease the normal unproductive tensions that go along with wedding planning, but therapy sessions can be a wonderful form of "foreplay" (whether you're first-timers and the wedding night will be the first time or you're old-timers and you're heading directly to the sack from the shrink's office). "Keep in mind that practically everybody gets aroused just talking about sex in a safe and productive environment."

The doctor says that although most men are comfortable telling their lovers what they want and like in bed, they are generally uncomfortable discussing their sexual desires—much less their sexual anxieties—outside the bedroom. As she mentioned previously, talking openly with one's partner is not only a way to deactivate fear of failure but an entirely erotic thing to do. As almost anyone involved in the business of sex will tell you, the single most erotic organ in the body is the mind—and I would like to add that the mouth (and we're not talking oral sex—it's more like *aural sex*) is literally the voice of the mind.

We certainly have no trouble considering speaking to a lawyer about legal obligations that come along with marriage. Nor is there any stigma associated with advice from financial exports. Many, if not most, couples meet with their ministers or rabbis before tying the matrimonial knot. So why not consider speaking with a marriage counselor or sex therapist? They understand the emotional terrain and can help couples navigate it better.

Dr. Pizzulli's Five Rules for Wedding Night and Marital Bliss

1. **Meet with a counselor or sex therapist before the big night.** It's not only rather stimulating to talk about sex in a safe context, but it will take the edge off. Any way you look at it, it is stimulating to talk about sex. No therapist? Talk anyway.

2. **Think about what turns you on.** The more you know about your own desires, the more you'll be able to communicate them to the person who will be fulfilling them for years to come.

(*Note*: Keep in mind that as much as men and women are different, we're also very much the same as human beings. I know it's not particularly manly to think this, but I do suspect that all men want to be thought as utterly appealing as the women we love are. Simply put, we want to have the same effect on them that they have on us. We live in a culture where male values and male desires and male bodies are generally not considered beautiful. In fact, the reality is often just the opposite. Perhaps that's why men tend to look at sex in such mechanical terms. Nevertheless, when we acknowledge that we want to be as lump-in-the-throat desired as the women we desire, we open the doors to a world of pleasures that we may never have considered were ours for the asking.)

3. **Pay attention to what turns on women in general.** Men's biggest mistake in the bedroom does not involve technique or an ability to sweet talk their sweethearts into bed. "A major impediment to sexual fulfillment, for both men and women, is to expect your partner to think or feel the way that you do. Men and women really and truly are different. Learn the differences. Respect the differences. *Vive le difference!* Then do some research on your own. Ask you fiance what turns her on. Ask female friends (without looking as though you're coming on to them). Dr. Pizzulli says that she has found that even though men generally dislike the program, we would be well-advised to watch several episodes of *Sex and the City* to find out how women think. And don't just watch the program—listen to what Carrie, Charlotte, Samantha, and Miranda talk about. Hear what they like and what they don't like. Pizzulli also suggests that men wanting to know what turns women on should consider that old 7up commercial where the women in an office converge at a window and drool over the construction worker taking off his shirt. She says women love to see men in traditional male roles. (And she also says that a white T-shirt doesn't hurt anybody's sexual appeal.) "Just pay attention," she says. It's not brain surgery.

4. **Learn about your partner's erotic hot spots.** You can't find out about them from magazines or self-help books or X-rated videos. You have to find out directly from her. She'll tell you or show you in one way or another; you just have to pay attention. Once you truly appreciate her for who she is—and respect the fact that she has different likes and tastes and desires than you do—you open the door to bliss. With all that in mind, you would do well to observe:

   a. *Her desire:* what makes her hot.
   b. *Her arousal:* what gets her aroused. It's different than what makes her desirous in the first place.
   c. *Her orgasm:* what brings her to climax. It's different than what makes her desire you or what gets her aroused. You need to observe and ask her. You need to understand that she will probably not be comfortable talking about them with you. Soooo...move on to number 5.

5. **Speak to her honestly and openly** about your own desires and anxieties. She will respond in kind.

Troubleshooting (or Trouble Shooting)

Just as Dr. Pizzulli recounted the story of her own wedding night—where she spent hours removing a hundred hairpins while her new and very drunk husband was passed out on the bed—stuff happens—or doesn't. Either way, there is only one reasonable response to bedroom troubles that first night: laughter. The next day, and in the months and years to follow, she and her husband had a great laugh about their unconsummated night—and as a result have had many more nights of wonderful consummation to follow.

"Above all," Dr. Pizzulli says, "don't make the first night mean too much." Whatever the problem, it's really up to you whether you turn it into a cancerous symbol of things to come or a great private joke between the two of you. The two of you now know a little more about how beautifully human each of you can be. "The intimacy of laughter between two kindred souls is as sexy as it comes."

Dr. Steinfeld, who has for years observed the healing effects of laughter and good humor on her clients, couldn't agree more. At the heart of laughter is the acknowledgement that we're all human—we're all bozos on the same bus. There are no superheroes in bed, just two people who love each other enough to lose themselves in each other's pleasure.

Dr. Pizzulli reminds men (and women) that sex is not only supposed to be fun, it is fun. Don't make it a battleground. Don't make it a contest. Don't bring anyone else into it. "It's the one wonderfully private connection between two people that never ever has to go anywhere else except between the two of you."

Above all, enjoy each other. Bring each other pleasure. That's what it's all about anyway. Right?

Chapter 14

Going to the Line:
Wedding Stories

The Sole of the Wedding

Leah Keith and I met as competitors in Orlando, Florida, where we were both on-air reporters. She worked for the ABC affiliate and I worked for NBC. We went head to head on most stories and somehow, despite our professional distaste for each other, fell in love.

We were to be married in June and her father was the only one who really cared about religion, so he wanted us to get married in a Catholic church. My family and I are not observant Jews, so that prospect wasn't daunting. I agreed. However, I did need to go through the pre cana conference in order to be allowed into the church Leah and I attended one in Fort Worth with 20 to 30 18-year-olds. Being almost 30 years old, we were so out of place.

The day consisted of lectures from accountants, family planners, priests, and others about the responsibilities of marriage and a new home. It was fairly progressive and easy until the last lecture. A gynecologist arrived and began his lecture on birth control. He displayed various paraphernalia and said everyone needed to ask a question before they were allowed to leave. The questions begin with the nuns and the priests in the back. I finally realized he was serious and needed to craft a question. I warily raised my hand to inquire about something to which I know the answer when he barked out, "I was wondering when you were going to come." I quickly replied, "Funny, that's what she said last night." Instantly I realized my Catholic indoctrination was in jeopardy. We were allowed to leave and Leah's family found the story hilarious if not bizarre.

That is the lead-in to the big day. All the families gathered in Little Rock for the occasion and my family sent more than 50 people, nearly outnumbering the locals. We decided it would be nice to have the local rabbi perhaps say a few words at the service and so we approached him. He said he didn't do that kind of service and wasn't interested. When he learned my family owns *The New York Times*, he said he could make accommodations for us and would be happy to have cocktails at his place with us the Friday before. We politely declined.

Friday night is the requisite bash and we behaved horribly. The next day I was barely able to tolerate a whisper when two of my best friends, Lucy Sullivan and Bella English, knocked on my door. They had come to commiserate. I was the last of our trio to get married and they wanted to see me one last time as a bachelor. We talked for a bit, they left, and I finished getting ready and headed off for the church.

The service began and, as required in all Catholic services, at some point we knelt. Leah heard it first, a titter from the audience. I began to hear the same chuckles and snorts as people suppressed laughter. I had no idea what is so funny, but it was very disconcerting. The laughter began on my family's side and gradually crossed the aisle to Leah's side. When we finally were married and left the church, the line of people laughing outside was quite amazing. My stepfather slapped me on the back hysterical and asked if I had any idea what happened. I didn't and when he told me all I could do was yell out, "Bella." She and Lucy had painted...*HE* on my left shoe and *LP* on my right in bright red nail polish, so when I knelt down, my shoes flashed...HELP.

—Dan Cohen
television production company president, New York, N.Y.

Who Is to Be Their Brother's Keeper? (How I Got Blamed for Ruining a Wedding)

My buddy (we'll call him Ben) came over to my apartment to tearfully relate his breakup with Olivia. They'd been dating seriously for more than a year, during which time I thought he'd become totally "whipped." So I met this sad news with unmitigated elation, telling him it was the best thing that could have happened to him, and that we'd all be able to go out, party, and chase girls. Thinking that it would make him feel better, I let him know that he could do much better.

This was my first mistake.

Predictably, they reconciled within the week, and suddenly I was on the outs for my exuberance over their breakup. Fortunately, I was able to repair the rift so well that I was honored by the appointment as best man at the wedding. I had never been a best man before, but I'd seen other weddings and movies about weddings, so I knew I'd give a speech, throw a bachelor party, and have a flask on hand to help the groom keep his courage up. Sounds simple, sounds fun, but it got complicated.

The bachelor party was fun, if not pathetically innocent. A week before the wedding all of the guys met to golf, go out for a steak dinner, and then have drinks out on the town. (I don't even remember a nudie bar visit or strippers.) We were in a shoreline city in the Carolinas and everything was working out great. The rehearsal went well, and the rehearsal dinner was a raging success. All the beer, wine, or sangria you could drink. And we did drink, heavily.

After clearly getting drunk at the rehearsal dinner, the question then became where we were going to party on Ben's last night of freedom. The first stop was to be the hotel bar, but my fiance stepped in: "You're too drunk as it is. It's Ben's big day tomorrow and it's much too important for you to blow it by being hungover—or making him hungover." Even through the sangria haze I realized she was right; and in the hotel lobby we parted ways with Ben and his brothers and stepsiblings. "See you bright and early," I said.

I woke feeling like hell. Got up, drank a lot of water, took some Tylenol and, because there was still plenty of time, I fell back into bed hoping that with a little more sleep I would dodge the hangover bullet. An hour later it appeared that although I took a hit, it was only a graze, no vital organs damaged, and I'd be okay for the noon wedding. I thanked my fiance for her sage advice, and I was feeling very fortunate that I didn't screw things up with a debilitating hangover.

All dolled up in the rented tuxedo, I jovially went up to the groom's hotel suite, where I was met by his brothers, who didn't look so good themselves. Turns out that after I left, Ben had been met by his college drinking buddies who, instead of letting him turn in early to sleep off the rehearsal dinner stupor, insisted that he accompany them to the bar where they proceeded to pour him shot after shot.

I subsequently learned that just before Ben was about to fall off the bar stool one of his brothers saw him looking a little green, and his siblings then brought him back to the hotel room where they plied him with more drinks and everyone had a great time.

To say Ben had a hangover doesn't do justice to the extent of his illness. He was suffering from acute alcohol poisoning, marked by severe nausea, weakness, and dehydration. It wasn't just that he couldn't keep anything down, he was actually on a regular vomiting schedule (every 30 minutes).

As the magic hour approached, Ben got no better. Upon arrival at the church, I scouted out private areas and bathroom facilities to make sure he could answer the call of the porcelain gods discreetly. Ben looked like death warmed over and I was there acting like a White House press agent distributing misinformation. The priest was told that it was a 24-hour flu that had unfortunately struck; a future brother-in-law remembered the plate of clams casino from the rehearsal dinner that must have been bad; and several others heard of Ben's extreme nervousness getting the best of him and his stomach.

After each bathroom visit I'd clean him up enough so that he was ready to marshal on like a good soldier, charging forward to certain death. Could he make it through the ceremony? Well, somehow he did—with knees locked; skin pale, cold, and clammy; hands shaking; and sweat on his brow. Ben managed to stay upright, and what's more, he did not vomit (I kept envisioning a projectile spray of bile launched onto the bride and priest).

However, after the ceremony, the receiving line was missing a groom, who was busy puking into the bushes on the side of the church. Afterwards came the endless photographs, which took twice as long as usual because Ben kept having to run (or wobble) outside.

Finally, the church was empty, save for the now impatient and disgusted photographer, the pitiable bride, her mother, and me. Just for the record, Ben's new mother-in-law is a short, humorless woman with librarian's eyeglasses and pageboy haircut. I was not about to say a word, but I couldn't help but notice her trembling in an effort to suppress her rage. Finally, she turned to me and hissed, "Well I hope you're happy, you've ruined my daughter's wedding!"

What do you say to that? I wanted to deny it ("Hey, I left early, it's not my fault, blame it on his college buddies"), but I said nothing. I realized at that point that my silence might be my most important function as best man. You take the heat for the irresponsible knucklehead because it's better that you're remembered as the ass instead of the new son-in-law.

It is debated to this day whether I dropped the ball by not staying with him until he was safely tucked away in bed. Perhaps I should have been the one drinking his shots for him, taking each one like a secret service agent is expected to take a bullet for the president. But I believe I did all I could and then some. Am I my brother's keeper? Hell, his own brothers were there and they let him suck down shot after shot. No, I did my job and took the criticism with a smile.

And everything turned out pretty well. By 7 p.m. Ben had finally recovered enough to do the Hokey Pokey at the reception. I gave my first best man's toast, not my best, but considering the added pressure, I was quite proud of myself. And no, I didn't reference Ben's over indulgence, his hangover, the gross kiss he must have given his bride, or the fact that I overheard the mother talking about "an annulment after the honeymoon…" and maybe her daughter "might meet a nice single guy in Hawaii."

—Rhett Weires
attorney, New Paltz, N.Y.

Everything but the Fish Bait

Karen and I had been engaged for almost three weeks, but had told practically no one about it. We picked up our marriage license at city hall in Manhattan, then went upstate to our cabin near the Ashokan Reservoir to wait the required 72 hours.

When all but three of them had passed, we called the justice of the peace. His wife answered the phone and called him in from cutting hay. We told him when our license would become valid and asked if he could marry us that day. He told us to meet him at town hall at 4 p.m., and to bring the license and two witnesses.

We had never thought about witnesses.

We frantically called everyone we knew within a couple of hours' driving distance. None of my friends were home, and my family was thousands of miles away. Karen succeeded in reaching two friends from high school and her mother (who then called Karen's uncle and aunt). I was able to get in touch with my college girlfriend (who had introduced me to Karen a dozen or so years earlier). We hastily told them where and when to meet us.

Town hall was also a state police barracks, and when we arrived the only car parked there belonged to the Conservation Department. No judge, no witnesses, not even a game warden. The sunny afternoon had assumed a distinctly unfestive gray demeanor.

As 4 p.m. approached, nine of us assembled in a room usually reserved for traffic offenders. Actually, we assembled in two distinct groups: Karen, the judge, and I made one little group and, well off to the side, everyone else made the other. No one wanted to stand too close to the judge—who hadn't taken the time to shower after working in his hayfield—but Karen and I didn't really have a choice.

We exchanged our vows while carefully breathing through our mouths. Five minutes later we were married, and rushed out into the fresh air (ostensibly to take some pictures). It began to rain.

We agreed to meet at the cabin for an impromptu wedding reception.

Along the way, we stopped at what passed in the country for a delicatessen in those days. By then it was pouring, and we had to run through rain-filled potholes to get to the store. All the store sold was bologna, white bread, beer, and jars of Uncle Josh's Preserved Porkbelly Baits and Salted Minnows.

We celebrated our nuptials with everything but the fish bait.

—Gary Allen
food writer, Kingston, N.Y.

Getting Hitched at City Hall

Noel and I had no engagement at all. We "had" to get married when we decided to adopt Jesse from Peru. Catholic countries don't look to kindly on the "living together" thing, especially when it involves a child. So off we went to city hall one morning and got married. Our reception was a bowl of congee (boiled rice with pork chop—Chinese breakfast) in Chinatown with a friend who was our witness. Then I called my business partner and told her I was running late because I just got married! She was quite stunned (she had the opposite...a really big, Jewish wedding) and couldn't believe we would do something quite that off the wall. Well, she was 12 years younger and was living the Yuppie lifestyle. We were still plugged into the 60s sensibility of "why would you ever want to have a big wedding." Ah, the generation gap.

—Margie Weiss
artist, New York, N.Y.

Watch What You Say, Especially to Your Mother-in-Law

Frankly, I didn't believe in the institution of marriage; I thought it was an outdated, conservative, and patriarchal establishment doomed to disappear from the face of the Earth forever, replaced by simple cohabitation with one's loved one. Nevertheless, I never should have said, "I will never get married"—especially not to my girlfriend's mother.

"Why would anyone get married?" I asked Suzy, Anne's mother, who was visiting with us in Berkeley for a few days. She was on her way to San Francisco with a belated wedding gift for her niece, Anne's cousin.

"Well," she said, after a moment of hesitation, "how about love?" She was no doubt bemoaning her rotten luck of having me as her daughter's boyfriend.

"Love is great, but why marry?" I answered self-assuredly. "You can just live together. Love will probably last longer that way."

"Well then," she tried again, "What if the girl gets pregnant? Shouldn't he marry her?" Anne and I had been living "in sin" for almost a year now.

"Not even then," I answered. "Two people can have the child and live together happily."

My future mother-in-law remained silent, perhaps contemplating how arrogant and stupid I could be.

It was the following Monday, only two days later, that I received a letter from the International House advising me that the University of California at Berkeley was required to send my name and address to the Immigration and Naturalization Service because my visa had expired. It was a new policy, they explained.

We were married on Wednesday, two days later, at 3:45 p.m., at the Alameda Justice Court. One day prior, Tuesday, I had called Suzy to announce that Anne and I would be getting married the next day, and that, of course, we wouldn't have a wedding (so no one was invited). She remained silent again, for a very long time.

It took about 10 years of "very good son-in-law behavior" to erase what I felt was an absolute dislike of me from my in-laws.

—Mihai Grunfeld
writer/associate professor,
Hispanic Studies, Vassar College, Poughkeepsie, N.Y.

The Room Makes the Difference

The wedding went off without a hitch. Our two families were from two distinctly different parts of the globe, but our two cultures got along perfectly. The weather was great and the food was outstanding even to this seasoned professional. It all started going downhill during the honeymoon.

We booked a package through our travel agent for a trip to Disney World. We thought we were getting a good deal on a "deluxe room" in a hotel that wasn't a Disney hotel, but was on Disney property and therefore had free shuttle bus access to all the parks and other attractions.

When we got to the hotel we quickly discovered why the room was so reasonably priced. The hotel was undergoing renovations. There was no carpet in the lobby. Our room obviously had not been painted in quite some time (scheduled to be renovated the next week, according to the management), and smelled like mold. Because we prepaid through the travel agent, we weren't able to cancel our accommodations and make other arrangements. It would have taken too long to get a refund and we didn't have enough cash to lay out for another hotel in the meantime.

Still optimistic, I tried to justify it all to my newlywed wife by saying things along the lines of, "We will not be in the room much anyway." My mother sent a beautiful flower arrangement to help righten the room and overpower the smell, but all was lost and the honeymoon got off to a really bad start.

After three days we finally decided to spend at least one night in a decent hotel, so we sat through a few time-share sales pitches and scraped up enough cash to get a room at Disney's premier Grand Floridian Resort. It would have been great...if only the car would have started. We actually wound up spending the day waiting for someone from the car rental agency to come and give us a new battery. We never made it to the Grand Floridian.

So here is a piece of advice for groom-to-be: The honeymoon is everything. Even if the wedding goes to pieces, you can still get it all back with a nice week away. Check those details and don't skimp on a room.

P.S. We stayed at the Grand Floridian resort about three years later when I had to be in Orlando on business. We even took one of the "honeymoon rooms." It was spectacular. I'm so glad we didn't make it there that one day because the rare taste of excellence would have surely spoiled what little fun remained on our beleaguered honeymoon.

—Dave Kamen
associate professor,
Culinary Institute of America, Hyde Park, N.Y.

Shangri-La

Exactly 29 years ago, Andy and I stepped off an airplane and landed in heaven. I knew that Shangri-La did in fact exist, but that its name was Bali. Still pristine and innocent, before the hoards of Aussies and Yanks chose to surf its shores and introduce the still bare-breasted and saronged natives to T-shirts; long before suicide bombers hurled themselves at dancing college students; long before the world's cultures collided and melted, we landed in paradise.

It was the most beautiful, romantic, exotic place on Earth. By day, we walked along terraced rice fields on the Agong River, swam in the ocean, and went to all manner of gorgeous ceremonies. In the evenings, we listened to gamelan music under thatched roof pavilions lit only by candlelight and torches, watched incredibly beautiful men and women dance in wildly colored costumes, and spent love filled nights in a Balinese hut on the edge of the ocean under the brilliant moon.

We were planning on getting married when we returned to New York, but the place felt so right, so beautiful, spiritual, and magical, that we knew we couldn't wait. We bought ourselves wedding rings, and typical Balinese wedding sarongs. We wrote our vows and chose our date: September 21.

On the appointed day, we went to the beach, and together vowed to cherish and respect each other forever, to live as one as man and wife. It was the most magical day in my life.

Two years ago, we returned to Bali. It is and will always remain the most beautiful place on Earth. And, of course, we revisited the beach and renewed our vows. Love endures in paradise.

—Penny Turkell
ASID: interior designer, Delray Beach, Fla.

Bad Omens

I should have known that my (first) marriage was going to be doomed when:
1. My best man was finally located three hours before the ceremony, passed out in his date's bathtub.
2. The best man wore sunglasses to hide his bloodshot eyes.
3. My future bride refused to be photographed getting ready.
4. My future bride was given away by a Norwegian farmer whom she met a week before.
5. She kept presenting her right hand for the ring.
6. Our reception was a beer blast that started two days earlier.
7. Folks at the reception threw bits of raw spaghetti instead of rice.
8. My brand new wife wasn't old enough to be served in the bar we all went to at midnight.
9. We had our wedding breakfast with eight other people with whom we'd been partying all night.
10. The reception was in Denver, Colorado, and the breakfast was in Cheyanne, Wyoming.
11. By the time we returned to our seedy motel room, we'd been married for two days.
12. The marriage was not consummated for two more nights.
13. The photographer lost the pictures.

—Tom Nolan
writer/technical support specialist,
Empire State College, New Paltz, N.Y.

Wedding-Revisited

After two attempts at trying to get a wedding off the ground, Denise and I were married on Ocracoke Island this past Saturday at noon.

I wanted something quite small with little fanfare, but was willing to go with whatever Denise wanted to do. After the original October 10 postponment, we decided to go for November 15. Some members of our families thought that there wasn't sufficient notice to make travel plans. I think that is what brought Denise around to deciding on eloping to Ocracoke. The bottom line was the fact that the wedding was being planned around all these other people, instead of us.

Anyway, we rode the Swan Quarter ferry to Ocracoke last Friday. The ferry from Hatteras has been suspended for two months because of hurricane Isabel. The two-hour-40-minute ride was very pleasant and romantic. Not many people have been going to Ocracoke. Eighty percent of the visitors to the island take the ride from Hatteras. When we arrived, we found the island practically deserted. It was peaceful.

After meeting with our minister, Ann Ehringhaus, for an hour, we scouted a location. It turned out that we chose a small maritime forest with a grove of beautiful old live oak trees. The next day at about noon we had our ceremony, with two witnesses (part time island residents) that we have gotten to know over the past few years. Also with us was John, our good friend, who let us use his house on the Pamlico Sound, where the weather was spectacular. The days were sunny and the nights starry. We had time to ride bikes, go clamming, kayaking, and just enjoy the warmth and solitude. It was wonderful, beyond any of my expectations.

John and our witnesses acted as our wedding photographers with their point-and shoot-cameras.

We returned home on Monday, after another nice ferry ride.

—Mike Halminski
wildlife photographer, Waves, N.C.

Part IV
Post-Game Wrap-Up

Chapter 15

The First Day of the Rest of Your Married Life

As this is our final conversation (before I turn the book over briefly to a few women for what might be reasonably called the last word on good husbandry), it has the feel of one of those ritualistic male moments where the men retire to the parlor after dinner and light cigars and pour some brandy and talk business...or if that's not your style, go down to the basement, have some beer, turn the television on mute and do some Monday morning quarterbacking...review the videotape...and think about what lies ahead....

Assuming you've been reading this book in chapter-by-chapter order, at this point you are already, in theory, a happily married man. You did it—or as they say in Brooklyn: you done it. Well done! And I might add in all sincerity, you simply could not have done better. After all is said and done in this life, we do what we can do, and then it is time to move forward.

Please know this: The days and weeks after a man is first married are, to some degree, the most elevating and confusing ones he might ever face in his life. He's happier than he has ever been, yet the world itself seems more complicated and sobering than he had ever experienced before in his life. And for no reason that he can figure out.

Despite the fact that the cultural laugh factory in which we live provides an incredible amount of choice material about newly married men crossing the half court line and, in doing so, leaving their boyhoods—and toyhoods—behind, getting married is no joke. It is a monumental vertical leap by anyone's standard, the LeBron of all major life transitions, in effect, making the jump from high school to the pros.

Moving to a New Arena

By formally choosing the company of a wife over the boys who have been with him through all those bad times and worse, a small part of every man suddenly feels a little alone out there on the court of his dreams. After tying the knot and returning to the court, he discovers that it's a whole new ballgame out there and he's not sure about all the rules, much less how he's going to perform. He's flying high and he's grounded all at the same time.

As an aside, few men in my experience have articulated it as well as newlywed Sean Schenker, who exclaimed to his father, Bruce, a few weeks after saying his vows, "I am now living in a girl's room!" One day, the lead singer of the rock band Mishap was living in a slovenly male paradise with his friends in Athens, Georgia; and then a few days later he had a floral bedspread, pink curtains, perfume in the air, clean plates in the cupboards, and a bathroom that would not be condemned by the Board of Health. Nothing had changed between Sean and Maegan, but everything had changed around him.

That said, the problem is not the change in surroundings. Life is change. Mishap broke up, Sean and Maegan moved to Brooklyn, Sean became a teacher, then found out he hated it, and started a new band named The Trapps. The problem lies squarely in the fact that because men are far less inclined than women to talk about their inner lives, few of us find the necessary companionship (as Sean did) to talk us through what could and should be a relatively easy transition game. In the absence of any male communication the weeks and months after getting your troth plighted, married life feels a little daunting to some men—and a perhaps even a little claustrophobic. And without a doubt, rather pink and frilly.

With that in mind, this chapter will include a couple of assists regarding communication and the newly married man. I hope they will make your transition game as smooth as silk—and might even help you feel a little less alone out there as you run through the plays on the court of your dreams.

Check the Scoreboard:
It's a New Game, but the Score Didn't Change

1. **You look the same as you always did.** You're balding—or you're not. You have love handles—or you don't. Your nose is still too big—and your biceps are still too small.
2. **She looks the same as she always did.** Everything you love about her is still there. Everything that you didn't love about her is still there. Right there.
3. **Your old problems didn't miraculously disappear.** You're still not getting along with your boss. Your brother still bullies you. You still can't drive left. You still get cold sores every winter.
4. **Neither did hers.** She's still afraid to be left alone in the apartment. She still doesn't get along with your mother. She still breaks out when she gets her period. She still doesn't like it when you belch.

As one not-to-be-identified newlywed told me, "All the baggage, good and bad—I'm just beginning to understand—will probably keep traveling with us until we reach the end of the line. It's who we are."

Staying the Course

The card up the sleeve...the ace in the hole...for every single guy in the universe is the unspoken knowledge that if any situation gets too dicey, he can always turn on the tube; pop the top on a beer; hit the bag; take a run; jump in the car; gun the motor, and disappear squealing around a corner.

It is not so with a married man. Right in the middle of that first marital squabble (and yes, of course, you will have one), many of you will be overcome with the knowledge that you will have to stay right there on the floor and deal with whatever offense or defense is being thrown at you. Even if you happen to storm off when the momentum is turning (slamming the door behind you, jumping in the car and screaming how you're "...never coming back here again!"), you will know in your heart of hearts that at some point you're going to make a squealing three point turn and drive home and take care of business like a man. You're in for the long haul.

And the long haul business of married manhood is simply (and not so simply) this: being able to communicate with a partner when you least want to communicate with anything other than your dog or your teammate on a fast break. It is an inclination and a skill in which men are given very little training as boys.

In a recent class of mine I asked the female students to list the most important qualities in the "man of their dreams." Included, of course, in some of their answers were the predictable qualities related to money and looks. But in this sample—and I assume anywhere else you would ask any woman in the world what her ideal man is like—every single response included the ability to communicate. (Interestingly, that was followed by having a sense of humor, which is the lubrication that allows communication to flow and which is where the second part of this chapter will take us.)

Keeping Up Your End of the Conversation

Communication is, as everyone knows, an essential ingredient to the smooth working of any partnership, whether it's a basketball team, a business, a share of a boat, or connection to your broker, your bookie, or the love of your life. Indeed, there may be nothing more important to the success of a marriage than being equal partners. That is not to say that you share equally in all the tasks of family life, but that you respectfully agree on how you share those tasks.

The problem, as you might have already figured out, is that in general, men don't particularly like to talk about feelings. Feelings are messy. They're gooey. And, by and large, we're not good at them. Not only that, feelings generally don't resolve themselves easily or at all. And, after all is said and done, men do best in situations where things are neat and concrete, where there is a winner and a loser, a right and wrong, a good and a bad.

So how do we learn to play the communication game when we are often so ill-prepared and poorly matched? First, keep in mind that talking about feelings is not necessarily communication. A lot of people can talk for hours about feelings without ever really communicating. In practice, a lot of feelings talk is "me talk"—that is, "I talk about my stuff and you listen." And second, there's a lot of good, healthy, meaningful talk that goes on all day every day that doesn't involve sharing one's deepest, most private feelings.

That's why talking *with feeling* about feelings is not necessarily the way to begin to learn how to be a good communicative partner. In fact, the discomfort with talking about feelings may cut off the conversation before it gets going. In the beginning of the relationship, learn to just talk about things that are real and involve both your lives. I suspect that feelings—and talk of feelings—will flow most naturally from that.

To push the basketball metaphor one more time, this is similar to learning how to use your left hand. You know you'll be a better player if you can go left to the hoop. You know you won't be as predictable nor will you be so easily defended. You'll bring surprise and added substance to your game.

The problem is that you can't just suddenly start using your left hand in a game. You've got to get to the gym and practice (and practice) going left.

First, Try Some Monday Morning Quarterbacking

First, you might practice your unused communication skills in a safe place: Get the juices flowing by jawing, however briefly, to your old man, your married friends, your married fraternity brothers, your married minister, your married rabbi, your married high school coach, your married colleagues—you get the drift, anyone you speak to has to be married. This is a fraternity you can't know squat about until you join it. And don't let anyone tell you differently. If they have not walked the walk, they don't have the language to talk the talk.

Everyone asks how it's going. Tell the chosen few in as few words as possible what you can about the confusing and conflicting feelings you're experiencing. Your response—and opening—could be as basic as, "It's different from what I thought" or "It's a little confusing." My guess is that most, if not all, married men jump at the opportunity to let you know that you are not alone. You might only get a nod or a grunt or a "Yup," but in most cases that's all you'll need to let you know that you're not the only one in the world feeling those feelings. Maybe one of them will even share a little of his wisdom on how he figured out what the confusion was all about (but don't count on it).

Stepping Up Your Game

Now you have to speak to the only one who really counts: your sweetheart. The most sensible and exciting suggestion I ran into for enhancing communication between newlyweds did *not* come from a shrink or a sex therapist or a marriage counselor, all of whom speak convincingly—but unconvincingly—about sharing intimacies. Ironically, the best advice came from the financial advisor, Ruth Hayden (see Chapter 8).

As you might imagine, Hayden did not once mention the palliative effects of couple classes...or the transcendental effects of the Kama Sutra...or the wonders of relationship therapy...or the salutary effects of creative visualization...or even the emotional profit of a massive portfolio. She spoke simply and convincingly of how "most couples need to learn how to be partners. Partners in values and goals." And better still, she backed up her ideas with an extraordinarily reasonable—and doable—approach to communication: the weekly money meeting.

The Weekly Money Meeting

Hayden explains, "There are three entities when we get married—you, me, and us—that each need to be cared for and nourished." The weekly money meeting insures that you're sitting down together and talking about a mutually important subject. Ultimately you're going to resolve issues and problems that drive other couples apart. It's a protective move, she says, adding that it takes an enormous amount of courage, to say, "C'mon let's just deal with it. We don't want anything to get us."

"In essence, couples need to talk about money because it's present, right in the center of their marriage, and, better still, it's all there in black and white." You can see how you're doing every week. Hayden says that the weekly meetings probably won't take any more than 30 minutes to an hour, but they will be the "best investments you'll ever make."

In the beginning, she suggests keeping it simple. Later on you can talk about the broader issues of a family budget. New couples should use the time to pay bills, which will give both of you a measure of intellectual and emotional ownership of your financial destiny. These weekly conversations will enable the two of you to get used to talking about money in small increments. They will encourage both of you to be on a common task. They will also give you ample time to practice money management and communication skills when there are no crises to get in the way; you'll be able to defer issues one to seven days rather than having to deal with them right in the middle of everything else that's going on in your lives.

Older couples might use the meetings to go beyond debits and credits, reporting to each other on various financial responsibilities and also to strategize. As discussed in Chapter 8, at these meetings you and your wife will actually have the information to consider important issues such as: how much debt you have, how much debt you want, under what circumstances you will use your credit cards, how much money each of you should put away from your paychecks toward the last 30 years of your lives, how much money should be put into a college fund, and how much mad money—or autonomy money—you should allow yourselves and each other.

Any way that you handle them, though, the regular meetings become a symbol of commitment to being a couple. "You're making time to make this relationship work." You're willing to have an open dialogue—you're willing to learn to talk more effectively—and you're willing to not always have to be right. Money becomes little more than a tool to make your values work and enable you to get to your goals.

And although some cynics might argue that money meetings take away from the romance of marriage, Hayden argues that the meetings actually take negatives about money out of the conversations between husbands and wives, and in the end, actually enhance romance and connection.

Managing Emotions

The key to managing money is managing emotions.

Nineteen years ago, Ruth Hayden told her husband at their weekly money meeting that her income was going to surpass his. She told him that if that posed a problem, she was more than willing to go to therapy but she was not willing to earn less money. "Well," he said, "we never had a belief in our marriage that whoever had the most money had the most say...and the way I figure it, we'll have more money and we'll still be us. What could be bad about that?"

Are the Weekly Meetings Working?

The critical factor is whether the agreement or system or aims is clear. There are two criteria:

1. Are we able to pay our bills?
2. Does it feel fair?

After her seminars, Hayden reports that "hands down, the thing that changed them the most were the weekly meetings. Their basic relationship changed and grew stronger. The essential element to communication is sharing space—that is, the ability to compromise—essential skill. Not losing—stretching."

Once the system is in place, she says, both partners should feel relieved and both feel uncomfortable. If not, someone is not stretching. "You might end up spending more (or less) money on vacation or gifts or retirement, but if the numbers work and it feels fair—uncomfortable but fair—then you have a heck of a deal and an excellent system to keep making deals to work for the two of you."

When the Money Runs Out: A Sense of Humor

It's tempting at this point to say something ironic or campy, something along the lines of what Dustin Hoffman's doughy uncle says to him after he graduates from college: "I have one word for you: Plastics." Or what my wife's 99-year-old grandmother Damma from Biloxi, Mississippi, told her about the meaning of life: "Family, Sense of Humor, and Real Estate." (More on that later.)

For now, if you happen to stumble into the amiable clutter we call a kitchen, you might want to check the busy refrigerator door for a cartoon of a rather harried-looking mother about to launch a child out the front door in a giant slingshot. It sits there yellowing in the messy midst of a hodgepodge of lost messages, crayon drawings, school pictures, last year's school menus, and 5-year-old homemade Halloween cards. Getting children out of the house on time (and onto elementary school bus or in college or to the wedding chapel or, later, into their own homes with their own families) has been the alpha and the omega of lives around here for more than three decades. It's the essence of the cycle of life as we have lived it. It's been wonderful, but it's also sometimes been exhausting, frustrating, humbling, dispiriting, and, on the darkest mornings, full of fear.

Nevertheless, Patti howled when I showed her the cartoon. I knew she'd appreciate it. I knew it would make her smile. As the saying goes, if we didn't laugh, we'd cry. Or worse.

Although some might say that I was being insensitive by poking fun at our family foibles, Dr. Steinfeld, smiles and affirms for me that the cartoon suggests we've been doing okay. By laughing at ourselves—and each other—she says we've found a healthy way to cope with the unavoidable stresses of marriage and family life. "A significant element in keeping engagements afloat is their ability to incorporate humor into their daily lives."

Dr. Steinfeld first noted a correlation between humor and healthy development in teenagers several years ago while doing doctoral research. In study after study she found that the healthiest kids had a high humor quotient. In contrast, unhappy or emotionally unstable kids tended to take themselves and their circumstances far too seriously. "They simply don't laugh as much as well-adjusted children. And that has significant effects on their physical as well as their emotional well-beings."

In her interview with me, she referred several times to a series of studies by Dr. Lee Berk at Loma Linda University School of Medicine, which demonstrated that laughter stimulates the immune system. A good chuckle actually lowers serum cortisol levels, increases the amount of activated T lymphocytes, and activates a lot of other physiological entities that most of us don't have the time or inclination to understand. In short, laughter makes us stronger. It also releases endorphins in the brain, which, in turn, create a sense of calm and contentment.

Steven Sultanoff, Ph.D., president of the American Association for Therapeutic Humor from Newport Beach, California, believes that expectations in the form of rigid thinking patterns make us less able to deal with challenge and disappointment. "And the ill-effect of mirthlessness is not just on adults. Children learn by experiencing their parents. They not only internalize what we do, they model it later on in life. If they see us moody and unable to let go of anger, they grow into moody and angry adults. If children see parents using humor in appropriate ways, they learn to develop therapeutic humor as they grow up. In effect, they learn not to sweat the small stuff and have a more healthy approach to life."

The question, then, is how do we learn to not sweat the small stuff? Especially if we're "humor impaired," as Leigh Anne Jasheway, the author of *Don't Get Mad, Get Funny* (Whole Person Associates, 1996) puts it. Jasheway, who teaches Stress Management at University of Oregon, says, "Too many adults are simply afraid to look childish. They prefer to look important and in control. Children laugh 400 times a day, but adults only laugh 15 times! We have to learn to see the world through the eyes of a child." What she means is that we have to program ourselves by integrating humor into our lives before, during, and after stressful situations occur.

The Calm Before the First Big Marital Fight

Jasheway believes that we can, in effect, store humor in a memory bank, to be drawn upon when we most need it. "It's like exercising, and you don't have to wear a leotard or running shoes." In fact, you don't even have to feel happy to laugh anyway and still get all the benefits.

Dr. Joel Goodman, organization founder and president of the HUMOR Project in Saratoga Springs, New York, and author of *Laffirmations: 1001 Ways to Add Humor to Your Life and Work* (Health Communications, Inc., 1995), speaks of building humor into the home environment. "To turn the farce of habit into the habit of farce." He suggests starting by doing such simple things such as putting cartoons on the refrigerator door or making a ritual of asking for jokes or a funny stories at dinner—and after dinner, perhaps watching a sitcom together. If the environment is full of humor, he says, "Laughter grows by osmosis into the notion of who you are as a couple and later as a family."

"Humor binds us together—especially those silly in-jokes that all couples share," Dr. Steinfeld reflects. "It levels the playing field for couples, and makes everyone feel a part of something larger than themselves. It not only insulates us from the outside world but keeps us connected. We have to learn to nurture that."

After the Squabble in the Movie Theater

Although couples commonly say after their own harrowing experiences, *This will probably be funny in 20 years*, Goodman wonders, "Why wait?" Why be miserable? Why take your frustration out on your spouse? When the dust settles on each of the endlessly predictable stresses in our lives, "Look for the comic vision, look for the funny stuff." And even if you don't feel like laughing, laugh anyway. It'll make you feel better.

I think Dr. Steinfeld says it best—keep the doors open to let in the laughter. Paste a smile on your face if need be. Laughter is the only real healer. (And I'd like to add that if you thought getting married changes your life, wait until you have a baby.)

Let's Go to the Videotape

One more thing: I mentioned earlier in the chapter that my wife once asked her 99-year-old grandmother, Damma, what the meaning of life is. She sat right up, looked her granddaughter in the eye, and said (as if she'd been waiting for at least two or three decades for someone to finally ask), "Family, Sense of Humor, and Real Estate." That's not a bad summation—at all.

Family is crucial to keeping us feeling warm and loved while we pursue our goals and dreams out there in the cold world. The longer you're married the more you'll understand that everything in your life is dependent on the health of your relationship between you and your wife. If it's not working between the two of you, every other area of your life will be affected.

And a sense of humor helps to keep us happy enough and humble enough to not let expectations get the better of us while we do battle out there in that cold world. If nothing else, a healthy sense of humor will help keep that most important relationship healthy as life predictably tosses the everything that is life right in your path. It will help you smile when you stumble—and laugh after you've fallen.

And finally, real estate: no joke. As I'm sure Ruth Hayden would concur, a little equity goes a long long way toward making anyone smile.

Chapter 16

What Makes a Perfect Husband

*A*s my favorite Existentialist, Albert Camus, wrote in *The Fall* (Vintage, 1991), "Somebody has to have the last word. If not, every argument would be opposed by another and we'd never be done with it."

Sounds reasonable enough. But then the question is, especially for newly married folks: who should get the last word? I suspect that Camus might say it really doesn't matter in the larger philosophical sense, but conventional wisdom (mostly gleaned from television and Hollywood) has it that the wife generally should and does get the last word in a marriage. Think Marge and Homer. Think Chandler and Monica. Think Hillary and Bill. Think Dave Barry: "Men are like a fine wine. They start out as grapes, and it's up to women to stomp the crap out of them until they turn into something acceptable to have dinner with." And don't discount the fact that most wives outlive their husbands, which really is the only way to finally get the last word on anything at all.

In the spirit of full disclosure, though, after 35 years of marriage, I must admit I have not quite learned the gentle art of leaving the last word to my better half. And, as you might guess, Patti agrees completely. However, that's not to say that I don't see the wisdom in women having the last word, especially in the context of teaching men to be good husbands. I mean, who better to tell us what women really want in a partner?

So, in a second spirit of full disclosure, here are some women who were kind enough and thoughtful enough (and in a few instances angry enough) to take the time and effort to come together to school us in what makes a good husband.

The Shoot Around

An archaeologist is the best husband a woman can have; the older she gets, the more interested he is in her.

—Agatha Christie
News reports, March 9, 1954

The secret to a "successful" marriage is, according to my husband, "Do whatever she says," and so I would say the answer to what makes a good husband is one who does whatever his wife says. It's worked for us for 50 years!

—Shirley Aigen
Spring Valley, N.Y., Married 50 years.

A good husband is one who is not so bitter that your former husband got to keep your dad's lifetime season Giants football tickets.

A good husband never asks, "How many sweaters do you have?"

A good husband never asks, "What the hell is that?" in reference to anything you've bought.

A good husband says, "That is a beautiful meatloaf."

A good husband will listen to four hours of Country and Western music drinking and cheating songs before saying, "That's enough," and putting on some Lou Reed.

During a blackout, a good husband finds all the candles in the house, including the box of Yahrzeits and the Mary Magdeline, lights them all, and makes a romantic evening out of it.

A good husband frequently inquires as to the health of your private parts.

A good husband, when sincerely implored, will get up in the middle of the night and wash his armpits.

After you've been ragging on him for 15 minutes, a good husband will loudly sing "Born Free" instead of popping you one in the snoot.

A good husband, upon spotting your gray sweatshirt in the hamper, will ask, "Does this go in with the light or the dark?"

A good husband gets out the Louis Prima when you're down.

A good husband always calls you "toots."

A good husband says, "I beg your pardon," when he belches. No, that's a lie.

A good husband never farts under the bedcovers. (See above.)

When you come in with your hair striped like a skunk or the color of strawberry sorbet, a good husband says, "That looks nice, toots."

A good husband is grateful to have one corner of a shelf in the bathroom for his Q-tips and razor.

A good husband says you're better-looking than your friends.

A good husband doesn't get jealous when you giggle over the phone with your male friends.

A good husband doesn't care that you got old.

A good husband takes directions well.

*And finally, a good husband takes off all his clothes, puts on a beret and a French accent when he wants to get you in the moo*d.

—Suzanne Murphy
New Paltz, N.Y., Married 18 years.

A good husband: he who has had numerous surgeries (all unsuccessful I might add) and has tried, and will continue to try, everything and anything on the market to cure the most annoyingly loud snoring condition that keeps his (darling) sleep-deprived wife awake every night, even though he swears he doesn't snore.

—Joan Altman
Katonah, N.Y.
Married to the same snorer for more than 25 years!

You may have heard this one in the movie Freida: *Freida's father, after commenting on how much he and his wife (Freida's mother) fought, was asked by his daughter, "What makes a good husband?" He replied, "A poor memory." Rump bum bum.*

—Nancy Austin
Elizaville, N.Y., formerly married

*Above all, it is a relationship.
It is having the ability to…
create special moments out of nothingness…
listen without judging…
give first, and then receive…
trust one another…and apologize…
respect each other's strengths and weaknesses…*

—Myriam Bouchard
Highland, N.Y.
Divorced from first husband in 1995,
Now with domestic partner since 1997

My first thought about husbands was:

A good husband speaks to you more often than your dog does.

Subsequent thoughts included:

A good husband turns on the bathroom fan as well as puts down the toilet seat.

A good husband, after volunteering to wash the dishes, washes at least two pans, a glass, a bowl, and a plate before wandering away from the sink.

And a good husband is actually honoring your goddess wisdom when he asks you to divine where his keys, wallet, and shoes are hiding.

—Brynna Carpenter-Nardone
Kingston, N.Y.
Married July 25, 1995 on a 95-degree day.

A good husband knows that some questions only have a wrong answer.

—Bonni Schenker
New Paltz, N.Y.
Married to Warren Gold for seven years

I don't ask much from my husband, do I? I may leave the house unlocked while we're gone for a weekend, but I don't want him to chastise me. When he tickles the baby till she shrieks, I badly want him to tickle me too. When I spend $1,000 of our money on shoes in a half-hour on the way back from Foodtown, can he keep his tone civil? My husband's job is like teaching nursery school—he has to be able to let me know when my flaws are not, as I instinctively believe, kind of adorable, but he has to include hugs and TLC, or I'll bellow out a tantrum that would frighten a bachelor off a balcony.

—Erica Casriel
Deal, N.J.
Married since 2000

My husband bakes wonderful multigrain bread by hand (bread machine is a four letter word in our house) every month. It is an irreplaceable staple in my diet, and I am eternally grateful for this.

I would also say that my husband thoroughly supports all of my interests and passions, whether they seem reasonable to him or not. We seem to be reciprocal on this trait, which works out quite well.

Oh yes, and while I'm at it, he also truly appreciates and enjoys the meals I make, even those that are more healthy than delicious.

—Julia Daniels
White Plains, N.Y., Married since 1989

I have come up with two definitions:
1. *Many modern women reject the very use of the word husband in favor of the term partner. By definition, as both word and archetype, a husband is a protector/provider; therefore, a good husband is one who is good at doing these things. The word partner evokes a more culturally acceptable equal frame. Common expectations, mutual trust, reciprocal communication, and shared responsibility are good partner qualities. As a modern woman, I heartily approve of the values implicit in the partnership model, and yet I admit, something there is (deep within the reptilian recess of my brain?) that hopes my young daughter will one day marry not merely a partner, but also a good husband.*
2. *What makes a good husband? My husband.*

—Tracy Gartelmann
Poughkeepsie, N.Y.
Married 15 years

The most important thing in a long-term relationship is the ability of my partner to acknowledge and accept the unpredictability of life. I couldn't stay with someone for a long period of time if he expected predictability.

—Jen Gentile
Single (but in a long-term committed relationship)

I once asked my mom if she had ever thought of divorcing my dad. "Divorce?" she answered. "No, never. Murder? Yes." I understand completely.

My favorite thing about my husband, Lee, is that he always makes me laugh, even in the middle of our worst fights. That was part of our wedding vows—to always keep a sense of humor—and we keep that promise pretty well.

—Dahlia Bartz-Cabe
Walden, N.Y.
Married since 1991

The Last Words

I think the perfect husband must have the intellectual capacity of Colin Wilson, author of The Outsider. *He must have the spiritual strength of Ghandi, the wisdom of Kahlil Gebran, the insights of Keirkigaard, and be able to cook as well as Peter Wolf. He must also be willing to clean up after himself, or at least pay someone to do it for him. He must be wise enough to realize that there will always be a "me" within the "we." I will not give up my dreams for anyone. He must never ask or expect any such sacrifice. Above all, he must be kind.*

—Dr. Sandra Cole-McNaught
Brooklyn, N.Y.
Married three times, currently divorced

A good husband is one that is willing (sometimes) to do things that he doesn't really like just because he knows you love to do them. Of course, this should work the other way around as well!

—Stacey Schenker
New Paltz, N.Y.
Married 35 years

I've passed it along to her—but her first response was, "How would I *know what makes a good husband?" Her implication was that her two husbands have been weighed in the balances and both been found wanting.*

—Karen Allen
Kingston, N.Y.
Compliments of her husband Gary

Marry a man who makes you laugh. Life makes you cry enough.
—Karen Mahon
Carmel, NY
Married 31 years.

He would cook and clean for fun.
He would fix cars but never talk about them.
He would detest sports.
He would never waste money on something as stupid as, say, a diamond ring.
He would be the smartest person I'd ever met.
He would have seen so many places and loved so many people that when we grew old we would always have something to talk about.
He would tell a good story.
He would never drink Coors Lite from a can.
He would play with my hair until I fell asleep.
He would pick me up in the sleazy local bar and pretend we had just met.
He would rescue me from most of the trouble he'd get me into.

—Laura McLaughlin
Gardiner, N.Y.
Unmarried

A good husband brings you the baby to nurse.
He also changes the toilet paper.
He also listens all night if need be.

—Polly Myhrum
Hughsonville, N.Y.
Married since 1971

A good husband loves you mind, body, and soul.
A good husband loves you unconditionally.
A good husband puts you above all else.
A good husband isn't just your husband.
He is your best friend, your companion, your soul mate.

—Amy Peer
LaGrangeville, N.Y.
Married seven years

The bitterest creature under heaven is the wife who discovers that her husband's bravery is only bravado, that his strength is only a uniform, that his power is but a gun in the hands of a fool.
—Pearl S. Buck
"Love and Marriage"
To My Daughters, With Love (1967)
(Buccaneer Books, 1996)

I have been divorced for a very long time so I am definitely not a good person to ask about marriage or husbands. If I ever was to remarry, the qualities that I would look for in a husband would be a very good sense of humor and honesty. It would be wonderful if I could be as comfortable with him as I am with my girl friends!
—Mary Ellen Potanovic
Raleigh, N.C.
Divorced

The perfect husband is a man who is willing to be adjusted when needed.
—Diane Sterling
New Paltz, N.Y.
Divorced twice

A good husband maintains a sense of humor. He will need it.
A good husband does not criticize his wife and definitely not in the presence of others.
A good husband learns to compromise.
A good husband seeks shared interests with his wife to further enjoy being together.

—Linda Maynard
Rodanthe, N.C.
Married 34 years

The best quality to find a husband is that he believes in the things that you believe in for yourself. Oh, another important quality in a husband is that he will take care of the stuff that you can't seem to bring yourself to take care of...like mailing the bills!

—Maegan Schenker
Kingston, N.Y.
Married 4 years

That's it, but in the spirit of getting in the last word, I have to admit I was tempted—just to be the 12-year-old boy who still lives in my soul—to end this with a thought from the great poet Rainer Maria Rilke:

> *A good marriage is that in which each appoints
> the other guardian of his solitude.*

—from *Letters to a Young Poet*
(Modern Library, 2001)

I actually do love the idea behind the quote and believe honoring privacy is an essential part of a happy marriage...but it certainly would be a sneaky, adolescent way of allowing a man to get the last word. So here's a final thought from a woman along the same lines:

> *All I ask, don't tell anybody the secrets I told you.*

—Lucinda Williams
from her song *Car Wheels on a Gravel Road*

And, of course...

I just want to say "Ditto" to Laura McLaughlin's wish for a husband who would cook and clean for fun. Mine doesn't see the fun in it.

—Patti Lewis
Married 35 years

Afterword

The following is the text of an interview that my old friend, Richard Gaynor, the best man at my wedding, conducted with his parents, George and Betty Gaynor, a few months after their 65th anniversary.

Betty and George are seated at the dining room table having tuna sandwiches for lunch.

Richard: Remember that book Steven is writing on marriage? Well, I think he may end it with you, or you'll be one of the last entries, and he's looking for a few secrets to your long, happy marriage, your formula.

George: (With that still-from-the-Lower-East-Side mischievous smile) He's gotta pay for that.

I tell him that's not going to happen, and move it along to Betty, while George asks, "How come this sandwich is so watery? Could you hand me another napkin, it's leaking all over my hand," We determine it's from too much lemon juice.

Richard: So, Betty...

Betty: (after very little thinking.)
   Patience. Flexibility. Sense of humor.
   (She turns to me.)

Should I say that thing about the phone bill? Never show your husband the phone bill, that helps to keep a marriage together. Is that all too serious?

Richard: No, it's just fine, it's what he's looking for. George?

George: I'm thinking…to love her, to try and make her as happy as I could, and to understand her problems if she had any. (He still looks pensive.)

Richard: Is that it?

George: That's enough. (He pauses.) Isn't that enough?

Richard: Yeah, that's fine.

I then read to them what they just said. When I get to the part where George said, "Try and understand her problems if she has any," my mother starts laughing.

"Try a little harder on that, especially today" Betty says.

Later, after George goes upstairs. Betty says, "He hasn't seen a phone bill in over 55 years, since he got home from service. When we'd get home from a vacation, and I knew the phone bill would be very little, I'd say 'Don't you want to see it, aren't you curious?' But he'd say no, he'd never give me the satisfaction."

And that's how it is, January 17, 2004, after 65 and 1/4 years of marriage. For the record, George and Betty Gaynor were married October 30, 1938, at the Senate in the Bronx. It was the same night that Orson Welles perpetrated his "War of the Worlds" radio hoax.

Appendix:
Crunching the Numbers

The Muggsy Bogues

	Prices ($) for 1/3 Carat (33 Points)									
Color \ Clarity	IF	VVS1	VVS2	VS1	VS2	SI1	SI2	I1	I2	I3
D	1843	1623	1492	1404	1272	965	833	614	482	351
E	1623	1492	1404	1316	1185	921	790	570	438	307
F	1492	1404	1316	1228	1097	877	746	526	395	307
G	1404	1316	1228	1097	968	790	702	482	395	263
H	1228	1097	1009	921	833	746	658	438	351	263
I	965	921	877	833	746	702	614	438	351	263
J	833	790	746	702	658	614	570	395	351	219
K	702	658	614	570	570	526	482	395	307	219
L	614	570	570	526	526	482	438	307	263	175
M	526	526	482	438	438	395	317	263	219	175

Example: 1/3 Carat, I2 (Clarity), G (Color) = $395

The Allen Iverson

Price ($) for 1/2 Carat (50 Points)

Color \ Clarity	IF	VVS1	VVS2	VS1	VS2	SI1	SI2	I1	I2	I3
D	5054	4056	3790	3325	3059	2593	2128	1463	1064	731
E	4056	3657	3391	3192	2992	2460	1995	1396	997	665
F	3657	3325	3192	2992	2726	2327	1928	1330	931	665
G	3325	3059	2926	2726	2394	2061	1729	1197	864	598
H	2926	2660	2460	2327	2061	1862	1529	1130	798	598
I	2327	2128	1995	1862	1729	1596	1463	1064	798	598
J	1862	1729	1662	1596	1529	1463	1396	997	798	532
K	1529	1463	1463	1396	1330	1263	1197	931	731	532
L	1463	1396	1330	1263	1263	1197	1064	731	665	465
M	1263	1196	1197	1130	1130	1064	997	665	598	399

Example: 1/2 Carat, SI2 (Clarity), G (Color) = $1,729

The Michael Jordan

Price ($) for 3/4 Carat (75 Points)

Color \ Clarity	IF	VVS1	VVS2	VS1	VS2	SI1	SI2	I1	I2	I3
D	8977	7182	6683	5985	5586	5187	4788	2992	1895	1197
E	7182	6683	5985	5586	5286	4987	4588	2892	1795	1197
F	6583	5985	5586	5286	4987	4688	4289	2793	1695	1097
G	5985	5486	5286	4987	4688	4289	3890	2693	1695	997
H	8286	4887	4688	4488	4289	3890	3591	2493	1596	997
I	4488	4289	4089	3890	3192	3491	3092	2394	1496	997
J	3591	3491	3391	3291	3092	2992	2793	2194	1396	897
K	3192	3092	2992	2892	2793	2593	2394	1795	1296	897
L	2593	2493	2392	2294	2294	2749	1995	1296	1097	798
M	2394	2294	2194	2094	2094	1995	1895	1197	997	698

Example: 3/4 Carat, VS2 (Clarity), L (Color) = $2,294

Appendix 215

The Larry Bird

Price ($) for 1 Carat (100 Points)									
Color \ Clarity	IF	VVS1	VVS2	VS1	VS2	SI1	SI2	I1	I2	I3
D	22211	14763	13167	11039	9842	8778	7847	5320	3724	2128
E	14630	13167	11039	10241	9443	8512	7581	5054	3591	1995
F	13034	11039	10241	9842	9177	8379	7315	4921	3458	1862
G	10906	10108	9576	9177	8645	7847	6961	4788	3325	1729
H	9576	9177	8778	8379	7980	7315	6517	5422	3192	1729
I	7980	7714	7315	7049	6650	6384	5719	4256	2926	1596
J	6650	6517	6384	6251	6118	5719	5320	3857	2660	1596
K	6118	4488	5852	5719	5586	5320	4788	3591	2261	1463
L	5453	3990	5187	5054	3990	4788	4256	3192	2128	1330
M	4522	2475	4256	4123	4921	3857	3458	2660	1995	1330

Example: 1 Carat, VS1 (Clarity), F (Color) = $9,842

The Shaquille O'Neal

Price ($) for 1 1/2 Carats (150 Points)									
Color \ Clarity	IF	VVS1	VVS2	VS1	VS2	SI1	SI2	I1	I2	I3
D	36708	25137	23142	19550	18553	16758	14164	8778	5985	3391
E	25137	23142	19550	19152	17955	16359	13765	8379	5785	3192
F	23142	19550	19152	18154	17356	15760	13167	8179	5586	2992
G	19750	18354	17556	16957	16159	14364	12169	7980	5386	2793
H	16758	15960	15361	14673	14164	12967	11172	7581	5187	2793
I	14164	13765	13366	12967	12369	11172	9775	7182	4788	2593
J	12169	11770	11371	10972	10374	9576	8778	6384	4389	2593
K	10773	10374	9975	9775	9376	8778	7980	5785	3990	2394
L	9376	8977	8578	8379	8179	7780	6982	5187	3790	2194
M	7980	7780	7581	7381	6982	6384	5785	4389	3391	2194

Example: 1 1/2 carats, VVS2 (Clarity), J (Color) = $11,371

The Yao Ming

Price ($) for 2 Carats (200 Points)										
Color	Clarity	IF	VVS1	VVS2	VS1	VS2	SI1	SI2	I1	I2	I3
D		70224	51870	45986	36708	29526	24738	20216	13034	8778	4788
E		51604	45486	36708	32186	28462	24206	19684	12236	8512	4522
F		45220	36708	32186	28994	27398	23408	19152	11970	8246	4256
G		35910	32186	28728	27398	25802	22078	18088	11704	7980	4256
H		30324	26866	25270	23940	22344	19684	16758	11172	7714	3990
I		23142	22344	21280	20216	18886	17024	14630	10640	7182	3724
J		19152	18088	17556	16758	15960	14630	13300	9842	6384	3724
K		15960	15428	14896	14630	14098	13300	12236	9044	6118	3458
L		13832	13300	12768	12502	11970	11438	10374	7980	5832	3192
M		11172	10640	10108	9842	9576	9310	8512	6650	5320	3192

Example: 2 Carats, SI1 (Clarity), I (Color) = $17,024

That's it. Follow this advice and you will end up with the ring of your dream girl's dreams.

Which reminds me that there's one more don't: *Don't ever* use the price of the ring to remind her of how much you love her. She'll never forgive you. For her, the ring is priceless. And it is.

Keep in mind that diamond prices fluctuate with the market. The grids are gleaned from several sources and only represent reasonable estimates of what your ring will actually cost.

Index

A

A list of guests, 82
A+ list of guests, 81
all-inclusive package for honeymoon, 136-137
Ambush, the, 20-22
autonomy money, 112-113

B

B list of guests, 82
bachelor party,
 a successful, 123-124
 10 taboos for the, 125-130
backyard wedding, myth of the cheap, 96-98
bad omens story, 185
baguettes, 31
Bali honeymoon story, 184

best man and the bachelor party, 125
best man, choosing a, 89
bills and cold feet, 116-117
blemish, 31
blessing,
 father's, 15
 what to say for father's, 16-23
 when to ask for father's, 16
blue-white, 31
brawling and the bachelor party, 129
bridal loans, 103
bride's parents and the bill, 94
brilliance, 31
brilliant, 31
Browning, Elizabeth Barret, 46
buying a ring,
 9 things not to do when, 26-28
 three things to do when, 29-30

C

C list of guests, 82-83
cake in the face, 161-163
carat, 31, 36
carbon, 31
carry-ons, 141
Carver, Raymond, 48
ceremony, etiquette at the, 159-160
checkbook questions, 112
city hall wedding story, 181
clarity of diamond, 34-35
cloud, 31
cold feet, bills and, 116-117
color of diamond, 34
communication and the newly married man, 190, 192-193
communication skills, practice your, 193
conversation and wedding night, 171
conversation styles of men and women, 107-108
cost
   for gonzo wedding, 101-102
   for medium-sized wedding, 99-101
   for small wedding, 98-99
costs of wedding, estimating, 96-98
costs, wedding, 93-96
Creely, Robert, 48
crown, 31
cruise for honeymoon, 136-137
crying and the bachelor party, 129-130
crying at ceremony, 160
culet, 31
cut of diamond, 33

D

date, groom's role in setting a, 79-80
diamond,
   clarity of, 34-35
   color of, 34
   cut of, 33
   flaws and the, 28
   shape of, 33
   substitute for a, 27
Dickinson, Emily, 47-48
disability insurance, 115
dispersion, 31
do-it-yourself prenups, 120
drinking and the bachelor party, 126-127
Dubin, Arlene J., interview on prenups with, 118-121
duties for The Day, 78-79

E

emotions, managing, 195
engaged man, job of, 71-70
engagement stories, 51-65
erotic connections, 170-171
etiquette
   at the ceremony, 159-160
   at the reception, 160-163
etiquette, the 10 commandments for wedding, 159-163
ex-girlfriends and the bachelor party, 128-129
eye-clean, 31

F

facet, 31
family, 199
fast break, the, 72-73
father's blessing, 15
   what to say for, 16-23
   when to ask for, 16
father-in-law, future, 23
fear of flying, 144-145
financial meeting, first, 111
financial pillar of marriage, 108-115
financing, 102-105
five rules for wedding night and marital bliss, Dr. Pizzulli's, 171-173
flaws and the diamond, 28
fluorescence, 31
flying, fear of, 144-145
four Cs, the, 33-36
full-cut, 31
future father-in-law, 23

G

gambling and the bachelor party, 127-128
Gaynor, Betty and George, interview with, 211-212
gemologist, 31
GIA (Gemological Institute of America), 31
   clarity grades, 35
   color grades, 34
gifts for ushers and best man, 90
girdle, 32
"good boy parties," 130
grand silent gesture proposal, the, 42-43
Grand Theft Auto, 17-20
groom's role
   in arranging for music, 83-85
   in arranging for tuxedo rentals, 85-87
   in booking a honeymoon, 87
   in getting a limo, 88
   in making a guest list, 80-83
   in planning, 77
   in setting a date, 79-80
   on the wedding team, 73-75
guest list, groom's role in making a, 80-83

H

Hayden, Ruth L., 109-110, 111-112
health insurance, 114-115
home equity loans, 104
home or renters insurance, 114
honeymoon
   and expectations, 131-132
   costs, 138
   is a bust, 146
   story, 182-183
   style, 133-134
honeymoon,
   groom's role in booking a, 87
   pack for your, 140-142
   when to go on your, 134-135
humor, sense of, 196-199
hurricane Isabel proposal story, 62-63

I

inclusion, 32
in-laws, story of meeting, 51-53
insurance, 113
   disability, 115
   health, 114-115
   home or renters, 114
   life, 115
   trip cancellation, 141-142
Isaacson, Julie, and the honeymoon, 131, 132

J

jewelry lingo, 30-32
jewelry on the honeymoon, 140
jewelry store, 26
jilted, being, 117
justice of the peace story, 179-180

K

karat, 32
Kossover, Andrew, 109
   and insurance, 113-114
   and the law, 116
   and the prenup, 121-122

L

lap dancing and the bachelor party, 126
laser-drilled, 32
legal pillar of marriage, 115-122
legal problems and your honeymoon, 145

life insurance, 115
limo, groom's role in getting a, 88
lingo, jewelry, 30-32
literary proposal, the, 45-48
loupe, 32
love, 150-151

M

managing emotions, 195
marriage partners, unlikely, story of, 153-155
married manhood, 192
medium-sized wedding, cost for, 99-101
minister story, meeting the, 56
money management, 109
money meeting, weekly, 194-196
mother-in-law story, 181-182
mother, your, 159, 161
music, groom's role in arranging for, 83-85

N

new age spiritual empowerment scenario proposal, the, 44-45
newly married man, communication and the, 190, 192-193
9 things not to do when buying a ring, 26-28

O

off-make, 32
Olds, Sharon, 48
Outer Banks proposal story, 60-61

P

partners, learn how to be, 194
pave, 32
pavilion, 32
pay-as-you-go financing, 103
people who have stake in wedding day, 158
playlist, choose your, 84
point, 32
popping the question, 38
prenup, reason not to do a, 121-122
prenuptial agreement, 117-122
   and assets, 119
   and living wills, 120
pressure on wedding night, relieving, 169-170
proposal story,
   April Fool's Day, 53-56
   hurricane Isabel, 62-63
   Outer Banks, 60-61
   series of close calls, 56-57
   show her the receipt, 61-62
proposal,
   sweet and simple, 49
   the grand silent gesture, 42-43
   the literary, 45-48
   the new age spiritual empowerment scenario, 44-45
   the sales pitch, 43-44
   the silent persuader, 40-42
   the utterly romantic, 49-50
   thematic, 39-40
   scripts for, 39-50
prostitutes and the bachelor party, 125-126

R

reception, etiquette at the, 160-163
ridicule from other men, 72
ring, the, 26
   ownership of, 116
ruining a wedding story, 177

S

sales pitch proposal, the, 43-44
scripts for proposals, 39-50
semi-mount, 32
series of close calls proposal story, 56-57
sex and the "wedding night," 165
sex therapist, 171
Shakespeare, William, 46-47
shape of diamond, 33
shaved head story, 57-58
sickness and your honeymoon, 145-146
silent persuader proposal, the, 40-42
single-cut, 32
small wedding, cost for, 98-99
Snyder, Gary, 48
sparkle, 32
Steinfeld, Dr. Marj, and popping the question, 38
suitcases, 140
support for women during wedding season, 73
sweet and simple proposal, 49

T

thematic proposal, 39-40
Three Card Monty, the, 22-23
three things to do when buying a ring, 29-30
10 commandments for wedding etiquette, the, 159-163
10 taboos for the bachelor party, 125-130
tiffany diamond, 32
travel
 consultant, 138-139
 package, 135
 troubleshooting, 142-143
travelers checks, 139
turn-ons for women, 172
tuxedo rentals, groom's role in arranging for, 85-87

U

ushers, choosing, 89-90
utterly romantic proposal, 49-50

V

vows, prepare your own, 91, 92

W

wedding ceremony speech, prepare a, 91
wedding costs, 93-96
wedding night as test, 167
wedding night troubleshooting, 173-174
wedding planning, 71
wedding season, support for women during, 73
wedding sponsorships, 104-105
wedding stories, 176-186
wedding suit story, the, 64-65
wedding team, groom's role on the, 73-75
weekly money meetings, 110, 113, 194-196

About the Author

Steven Lewis is a freelance writer, college mentor, devoted husband, Zen dad, and, according to Melissa, Michael, Jon, and Jeffrey, a pretty easygoing father-in-law. He is the author of *Zen and the Art of Fatherhood* (Plume, 1997), *The ABCs of Real Family Values* (Plume, 1998), and hundreds of magazine and newspaper articles on family life. Having been happily married for 35 years, in which time he has survived more than his share of engagement and wedding missteps, bought a whopper of an anniversary diamond for his sweetheart, and planned and paid for the weddings of three daughters, Steve has come to know practically everything a man should know about engagements, weddings, and the roots of domestic bliss. He and his large family live in the green shade of the Shawangunk Mountains outside of New Paltz, New York.